CW00467819

A Storm in the Wassail Bowl

A Hal Westwood Restoration Mystery

Christmas 1663

by Jemima Norton

TUDOR GATE PRESS

LARGE PRINT EDITION

Copyright © 2004 Tudor Gate Publishing Ltd.

All rights reserved, including the right of reproduction, in whole or in part, in any form.

ISBN 0-9740949-1-9

Large Print Edition

For ordering information contact:
www.tudorgatepress.com

THIS BOOK IS DEDICATED TO

Irene
&
the original Jemima

CHARACTERS

THE JOLYONS

Sir Edward Jolyon,
aged 57 — *Lord of Sidworth Castle*

Lady Mary Jolyon,
24 — *his wife*

THE SOAMES

Walter Soames
45 — *Sir Edward's cousin and heir*

Avis Soames
42 — *wife of Walter Soames*

Geoffrey Soames
22 — *son of Walter Soames*

THE ARMSTRONGS

Guy Armstrong
27 — *a neighbour of Sir Edward*

Fanny Armstrong
25 — *Guy Armstrong's sister*

Cecily Armstrong
15 — *Guy Armstrong's sister*

THE WESTWOODS

Hal Westwood 23 — *Lady Jolyon's brother*

Libby Westwood 22 — *Hal Westwood's wife*

Ned Westwood 17 — *Lady Jolyon's brother*

Bess Westwood 18 — *Lady Jolyon's sister*

Harry Westwood 2½ — *Hal Westwood's son*

AND ALSO...

Justin Danvers 20 — *Libby Westwood's brother*

Zac Drew 49 — *constable, blacksmith and St George*

Tom Greene 45 — *ale draper and dragon*

Alice 52 — *cook at Sidworth Castle*

Meg 24 — *Lady Jolyon's woman*

Thomas Featherstone 39 — *curate of Sidworth; betrothed of Fanny Armstrong*

Humphrey 58 — *servant of Sir Edward*

Alys 28 — *servant of Libby Westwood*

GLOSSARY

BD   *Brewer's Dictionary of Phrase & Fable*

OED *Oxford English Dictionary*

akimbo	with body curved or crooked and arms thrown out *(OED ME)*
ale draper	keeper of an ale house *(BD 1593)*
benighted	night fall; to be overtaken by night *(OED 1560)*
boobie, dolt	a dull, heavy stupid fellow *(OED 1543)*
Borgia's brew	an allusion to Lucretia Borgia, daughter of Pope Alexandra VI, who was notorious as a poisoner *(B D)*
brought up his boots	colloquism for vomiting
buss	a kiss *(OED 1571)*
camlet	mix wool / camel hair / silk fabric *(OED 17C)*
chap fallen	chap ; lower cheeks & jaw ; open-mouthed idiots *(OED 1555)*

chatelaine	girdle
churl	a rude, lowbred fellow *(OED ME)*
cipher	one who fills a place, but is of no importance *(OED 1579)*
closet	a small private room off a larger chamber *(OED 1601)*
court cupboard, buffet	a moveable cupboard used to display plates
Court of Arches	an ecclesiastical court of appeal (BD)
crab apple	the name of a wild apple *(OED ME)*
crowner	coroner *(OED ME)*
death's head at the feast	an allusion to the ghost of Banquo in *MacBeth* by Wm Shakespeare
draggle-tail	one whose skirts trail in the mud; by implication a woman of ill-repute *(OED 1596)*
flannel	open woollen stuff of loose texture *(OED 1503)*
gallery	a long narrow corridor *(OED 1541)*
Great Hall	the large hall of a castle

greensick	an anaemic disease affecting young woman at puberty giving a pale greenish cast to face *(OED 1583)*
grizzled	having grey hair *(OED 1606)*
groat	a coin worth about 4 pence in use 1351–1662 *(OED)*
helm	a helmet *(OED OE)*
Herne the Hunter	a spectral hunter of legend who inhabits wild forests *(BD 16th c)*
jackanapes	a pert, vulgar, apish little fellow *(BD 16th c)*
jade	a term of reprobation for a woman
midden	dung heap *(OED ME)*
Molly	a pet form of Mary *(OED 1567)*

mummers	disguising and taking part in a mummer's play	*(OED 1465)*
noisome	ill smelling	*(OED 1577)*
notions	ideas	*(OED 1567)*
philtre	a love potion	*(OED 1587)*
poesy	poetry	*(OED ME)*
pox	syphilis	*(OED 1503)*
privy stair	private or back stairs	*(OED ME)*
prosaically	plain, simple or matter of fact; hence dull & commonplace	*(OED 1561)*
puckish	mischievous or impish	*(OED 16th c)*
purblind	quite or totally blind	*(OED1615)*

rake   a man of loose habits and minimal character ; an idle, dissipated man of fashion   *(OED 1653)*

stews of Southwark   Southwark was an area on the south bank of the Thames in London notorious for its brothels a stew is a brothel   *(OED ME)*

square the circle   to attempt the impossible

settle   a long wooden bench used with high back and having box under arms   *(OED 1583)*

soughing   to make a rushing, rustling or mur muring sound of the wind   *(OED OE)*

slug-a-bed   one who lies long in bed through laziness

solar   a small withdrawing room of hall of castle   *(OED ME)*

Sycilla & Charybdis
alludes to the danger of avoiding one peril to fall to another ; a dangerous whirlpool on coast of Sicily opposite Italian rock Scylla *(OED 1597)*

sweet meat
sweet food; sugar cakes; candied fruits; sugared nuts; *(OED ME)*

stone
a unit of measure equal to 14 lbs avoirdupois

tester-bed
a canopy over a bed supported on post of bedstead or ceiling *(OED 1622)*

vouchsafe
to give grant or bestow in acondscending manner *(OED1671)*

Yule log
large log burnt during festival of

wise woman
a woman skilled in magic or hidden arts; a witch; sorceress; especially a harmful or beneficent one who deals charms against disease, etc.(B D)

woodwild
one who has lived alone in the woods too long and lost their wits

ENGLISH FEAST DAYS

Corpus Christi *Mid- June*

St. Stephen *December 26th*

May Day *1st of May*

Lammas *1st of August*

Twelfth Night *feast of the Magi, Epiphany*

ENGLISH QUARTER DAYS

THE DAYS WHEN RENTS WERE DUE

Michaelmas St Michael's Day
29th September

Christmastide Christmas Day
25th December

Lady Day Feast of the Annunciation
25th May

Mid- Summer Day
24th June

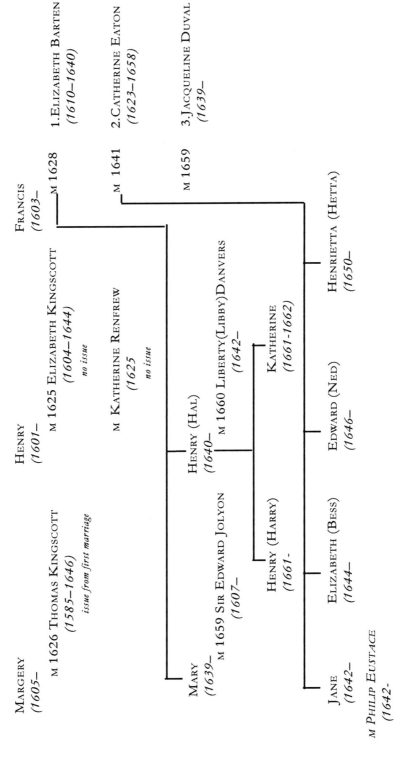

THE WESTWOOD FAMILY TREE
SIDWORTH CASTLE CHRISTMAS 1663

MARGERY
(1605–

m 1626 THOMAS KINGSCOTT
(1585–1646)
issue from first marriage

HENRY
(1601–

m 1625 ELIZABETH KINGSCOTT
(1604–1644)
no issue

m KATHERINE RENFREW
(1625
no issue

FRANCIS
(1603–

M 1628 — 1.ELIZABETH BARTEN
(1610–1640)

M 1641 — 2.CATHERINE EATON
(1623–1658)

M 1659 — 3.JACQUELINE DUVAL
(1639–

MARY
(1639–
m 1659 SIR EDWARD JOLYON
(1607–

HENRY (HAL)
(1640–
m 1660 LIBERTY (LIBBY) DANVERS
(1642–

HENRY (HARRY)
(1661-

KATHERINE
(1661-1662)

ELIZABETH (BESS)
(1644–

EDWARD (NED)
(1646–

HENRIETTA (HETTA)
(1650–

JANE
(1642–
m PHILIP EUSTACE
(1642-

Hal Westwood Restoration Mystery Series

BOOK 1

A Flutter in the Dovecote

Summer 1660

Refresh your memory by re-reading the Final
Chapter of this book beginning on page 284

BOOK 2

A Storm in the Wassail Bowl

Christmas 1663

BOOK 3

A Trip to Jericho

Summer 1665

Enjoy the First Chapter
of the next book in the
series beginning on page 292

Chapter One

Hal Westwood pushed aside the leather curtain and pulled a long face as the coach lurched into yet another pothole and came to rest at a drunken angle. The men got down wearily, muttering under their breath.

"Is it much further?" Libby asked, sitting herself up yet again and rocking the little boy, who showed signs of waking.

"I had thought not," he replied grimly, "but looking at the state of this road we could even yet be benighted."

"Oh Hal, I do hope not," she cried anxiously glancing to the child's nurse, whose faced mirrored her fears.

"I'll get out and take a look." Ned was restless. He opened the door and let in a blast of cold, damp air.

"Be careful of the—too late!" Hal sighed and leaned back wearily against the cushions of the coach. "I knew this would be a mistake. Visiting at this time of the year is always fatal. You realise, if it should snow, we could be trapped for weeks!"

"It hasn't snowed at Christmas for three years, Hal," Libby replied calmly.

"Not at home perhaps, but in these western hills," his doubtful glance strayed again to the lowering sky. "I hope nothing goes wrong," he added lowly.

Libby's smile was tender. "Oh Hal, you have got the glooms," she teased. "Why on earth should anything go wrong?"

He glanced back into the dim interior of the coach, a rueful expression coming to his handsome face. "Oh, I don't know," he replied vaguely. "Perhaps it's no more than the ache in this cursed shoulder of mine, but I have the oddest feeling. I am filled with foreboding."

Libby, who knew her husband well after three years of marriage, gave him a loving smile. He was still, in her eyes, a very handsome man. He was tall, lithe, with dark, fashionable colouring and blue eyes, which lit up his face when he smiled. Unfortunately he wasn't smiling now, nor had he for several weeks, she remembered, with a rueful grimace. Not since he had injured himself. "It's because you've been cooped up in here too long. You and Ned are both as bad as each other, in that respect. You hate to travel by coach."

"Aye," he agreed, "but needs must."

"Yes," she murmured, kissing the silken hair of her son.

"Poor Mary needs the support of her brothers."

"It will be good to see Mistress Bess again, too," said Alys the nursemaid.

Hal smiled his agreement. "I must confess I've missed her greatly. Ah, here comes Ned." He pulled back the curtain more fully. "What news, Ned?"

"The Castle's no more than a mile along this road," he announced, his freckled face reddened by the wind. "The village is just beyond the bend there, but the road, if anything, gets worse. It will take William and John all of an hour to move this coach. The wheel, if it isn't broken, is caught fast against a rock." He looked beyond his brother to Libby. "Does Harry still sleep? I am of the opinion it would be better if we walked. It seems there are no vehicles to be had in the village, and all the horses are out at the hunt, but I think we could be there in half an hour or so, if we walked."

"I'll carry Harry." Hal was glad of the chance of some exercise. He opened the door and jumped down, regardless of the mud splattering his fine leather boots. "Let me take him, Libby."

"Mind the mud Hal!" she protested and glanced from his feet in horror, to the pitted and rutted lane, which stretched away, muddied in the distance. Carefully she handed the sleeping child down to him.

"It's not so bad if we keep to the grass along the side," said Ned, coming to hand her and the nurse down. "And I'll carry little Harry, Hal. The weight of him will drag on your weak shoulder."

Seeing there was no help for it, Libby hitched up the skirts of her heavy travelling clothes and joined them in the lane. A cold wind whipped at her hood, snatching it from her hair and leaving her head and face exposed to the tiny needles of rain that filled the air.

"Do keep Harry covered, Ned," she cried, twitching her hood back into place. "He'll catch cold if he is wetted." Hal pulled a fold of Ned's thick, fur-lined cape about his little son, and offered his wife his sound arm. With the maidservant carrying their more essential items following along behind, they set off in the direction of the castle.

It was a full hour later, when the short winter's day was coming to a close and dusk fast falling, that they finally made their way up the steep path and under the ruinous gatehouse of Sidworth Castle. They crossed a moat, which appeared to have accumulated the rubbish of generations, and came into a courtyard remarkable only for its damp, desolate air and lack of life.

"Do you think this is the right place?" asked Libby in a whisper, as she looked about her uneasily.

"Yes," said Ned, with calm certainty. He advanced to a huge oaken door, which bore the scars of countless dogs scratching at it, and pulled at a rusted bell, which hung alongside. The abrupt clamour echoed in a ghostly manner about the dank, darkened courtyard, awakening the child who sat up with a cry of fear. "Shush, Harry," soothed Hal, although he, too, glanced about in dismay.

Then as they were exchanging disconcerted glances and wondering what to do next, a window was thrust open high above them, and a pale-faced young woman with long, brown hair looked out.

"Hal," she cried joyfully, espying her brother. "Hal, Ned, and Libby too!"

"There, I told you it was the right place," cried Ned. "Open up, Bess, do, we are soaked to the skin and Libby's half-dead with cold and fatigue."

"Where is your coach? I've been sitting watching for your coach this hour past. No, never mind, I'll come down. It could be ten minutes before that idle Humphrey stirs himself to answer the door."

The shutter closed with a slam and they waited in hopeful silence for their sister to reappear. The sound of raised voices came from within and all at once the door was pulled open to reveal not only Bess, but Mary too, with a curious maidservant lurking in the background.

"Welcome Hal," cried Mary. "Oh, you must be half-frozen! Ned." Fiercely she hugged and kissed her younger brother, making the colour rush to his cheeks. "It is years since I last saw you. Oh, how you've grown! Why, you are nearly a man."

"I am a man," he retorted gruffly, extricating himself from her embrace. "I'll be eighteen come Lammas."

"Mary, this is Libby, my wife," said Hal, as Libby emerged from Bess's fond embrace and was assisted from her wet cloak.

"I am pleased to meet you, Lady Jolyon." Libby was stopped halfway in a curtsey and found herself enfolded in another pair of arms. She scarcely had time to notice how her hostess trembled so violently.

"Call me Mary, please. We are as sisters, there must be no ceremony amongst us. Oh, I am so glad you are all come!" She smiled tremulously upon them. "Are we not joyful, Bess?"

"Oh yes," said Bess, coming to relieve the nurse of her sleepy burden. "Oh, how little Harry has grown, Alys," she cried hugging him. Harry, who had not seen his aunt in many months, hid his face bashfully.

"Come to the fire," cried Mary as Hal and the nursemaid were also divested of their wet cloaks. "Tell me, how is it you came on foot? Where is your coach? Meg, where is that mulled wine, I bade you bring?"

"I'll fetch it now, my lady," replied the girl pertly, fluttering her lashes at Hal.

"That girl is hopeless," said Mary shaking her head. "She seems to spend her days in a dream. Either that, or she's putting ribbons in her hair. It is time I saw her wed to some man who'll give here more to think about. But come you to the fire and warm yourselves, you must be chilled to the bone."

The Great Hall, as they entered, was impressive, rising up through three floors to be lost in the dimness. It was large enough for them to feel both dwarfed and insignificant, and anything but welcome. It was also cold, with very little warmth coming from the fire at the far end, under an age-blackened chimneypiece. The massive stonewalls were bare, but for tattered and rotting tapestries and heads of various beasts of the chase hanging there. The candles, lit already to combat the gloom of the short winter afternoon, did little to cheer it, and there was an over all pervasive smell of damp. It made Libby shudder and make a mental note to see that little Harry was kept warm at all times.

"We abandoned the coach in the lane." Ned ushered

Libby to the fire, which burnt smokily. The ingle-nook, which was the breadth of the dim hall, was large enough to take the half a tree trunk smouldering there. "The potholes on the road from Helchester proved too much for it."

"Oh yes, the road is very bad. Bess says it is quite dreadful this year." Mary faltered over the words. "Edward should really do something about it, but he says he—" she broke off, blushing a little and added with a bright, would-be-confident smile, "and he, of course, never travels by coach, but rides everywhere."

"Yes, so do I usually," replied Hal with a rueful half-smile. He added politely "Is Sir Edward from home?"

"Yes—yes, he—he had an appointment with—with —but he will surely be returned by suppertime," she ended swiftly.

"We shall be happy to meet him then," replied Hal. He was polite, but a slight stateliness entered his voice.

"Indeed, ah, is this your little son?" she asked as Bess finally released the struggling child from his confining blankets and set him, as he desired, to the floor. "Oh, but he is strong and well grown. Is he yet two?"

"Yes, back in the spring," said Libby proudly as he ran to her and clung to her skirts. She lifted him to her lap and smoothed back his damp, dishevelled hair with a loving hand. "I fear he is a little shy of strangers," she added apologetically.

An elderly woman, dressed in a gown of drab blue in the old-fashioned manner, came down the stairs. Age had not padded this woman's frame, her build seemed to echo her conscience; they were both upright and rigid. Her clothes, which were more of those of ten years before, when the Lord Protector, Oliver Cromwell, ruled the land, hung from her shoulders limply. Her pale blue, lacklustre eyes looked over the group before the fire grimly, and her colourless lips stretched into a smile, which held as little warmth as the fire.

"I am no stranger," protested Bess, as the woman approached. "Come Harry, you cannot have forgotten your Bess."

"Hal, Libby, let me make you known to my husband's kinswoman, Mistress Soames," said Mary, with a marked lack of enthusiasm, as the woman crossed to join them at the hearth. "Cousin Avis, these are my brothers, Hal and Ned Westwood and Hal's wife, Libby."

"God give you health, good Sirs and Mistress," replied the woman. Her eyes went to the child on Libby's lap, whom Bess was trying to tempt away with a sweetmeat. "I trust your journey was uneventful."

"Hardly that, but we are arrived now, I thank you." replied Hal, as the serving girl came finally with the mulled wine, in mugs wrapped about by pieces of flannel.

Seeing her guest engaged with her brothers, Mary went to admire the little boy. "My, but he is a handsome lad," she said patting his silky curls. "You must be very proud Libby, and Hal must be pleased to have secured an heir."

"We are most thankful to have him," Libby agreed, smiling as the child finally overcame his shyness, and slipped from her lap into Bess's arms to secure his marchpane. She laughed indulgently, and then glanced to her hostess. "Have you many gathered here to celebrate Christmastide?"

"Apart from those of my own family, who are doubly welcome," said Mary. "we have Sir Edward's kinsfolk, Walter Soames and his wife." She nodded in the direction of the woman Hal was listening to with polite attention.

"And their son Geoffrey. Walter is Sir Edward's heir," she added, a shadow crossing her face. "He comes each Christmas and other times, too. Then we have our neighbour and good friend Guy Armstrong, who has brought his two young sisters, one of whom is betrothed to the rector of Sidworth, and perhaps another one or two guests." She glanced uncertainly to Bess.

"A full table then," said Libby politely.

"Not so full as I had wished. I did write to Jane to beg her and her husband might join the company, and Father and Jacqueline, too. However, it was not to be, and as my husband has not been in full health lately, perhaps it is as well." She smiled briefly. "A small company can keep Christmas as well as a large, they do say, although I do like to see all of a family gathered to celebrate."

"What, even if it does lead to quarrels and bad feeling?" Ned asked turning aside and taking a further sip of his wine.

"Aye," Hal grinned. "You should have been at Westwood last Twelfth Night, Mary. Our dear stepmother still knows how to raise the dust."

"Have you not seen Father since last Christmas then, Hal?" asked Mary.

"I met him in London in May when we—" he stopped abruptly, glancing awkwardly to his wife.

"When he broke off Bess's betrothal to Libby's brother?" asked Mary.

"London is an ungodly place," announced Mistress Soames. "It is a pit of hell filled with strumpets and drabs, who tempt men to lust and evil."

"There never was a formal betrothal," said Hal shortly, as Mary cast a look of dismay at her husband's kinswoman.

"I'm sure Bess considered it a betrothal," Mary said quickly, casting her sister's bent head a sympathetic look.

Hal shifted uneasily in his seat. "Bess is too dutiful a daughter, I am sure, to do so," he replied with firmness. "Our father knows best what marriages suit his children."

"Our Father knows best how to keep all his children from sin, if we would but heed Him," said Mistress Soames devoutly.

"That's all very well for you, Hal," snapped Mary, casting a distracted look at the older woman. "Happily married as you are, but small comfort to those of us sacrificed at the altar of father's ambition."

"I charge thee—put away ambition—that way the angels fell!"

"Lord!" Ned muttered irreverently under his breath. He was unable to take his eyes from Mistress Soames, but Hal's face darkened with annoyance at this outspoken criticism from Mary, and even Bess looked shocked.

Libby, taking in the volatile situation, rose to her

feet hastily. "Forgive me, Mary," she said quickly, before her husband could speak the hasty words that would spell doom to a peaceful Christmas. "I do think we should all change from these wet garments before we take our death of cold."

"Death is cold—as cold as the grave!" said Mistress Soames ghoulishly.

"Good heavens, yes," cried Mary, her high colour fading. "I beg your pardon. What have I been about, to keep you standing talking in wet clothes? Come Libby, I'll show you to your chamber. Pray excuse us, Avis."

Mary hastily led them away, Bess following with Harry in her arms. She said nothing further, hurrying along out of the Hall, across another smaller chamber, into a long corridor, until at the foot of a flight of wide handsome stairs, she turned and said quietly, "I beg your pardon for my husband's kinswoman. Sometimes she is gripped like that and one hardly knows what to say to her."

"Is she mad?" asked Ned bluntly, his young face alive with curiosity.

"Oh no, no! She is quite harmless, only rather religious, and strict in her notions. Edward says she should have been a nun. Now, I decided to put you all in the tower rooms, for you'll be more private there and, provided the wind doesn't blow from the east, quite comfortable." Mary continued to talk even as she climbed the stairs, her voice hushed yet rapid, as if she were afraid somebody might overhear her words.

"What happens when the wind blows from the east?" asked Ned, now even more curious.

"The chimneys smoke, well, they all do really. Not just in the tower, but it's much worse when the wind comes from the east," said Mary with an uneasy smile. It seemed to Libby she was ashamed of the shortcomings of her home.

She led the way quickly along a wide, ill-lit passage, panelled in dark wood and striking chill to them in their damp clothes. They arrived finally at the base of a flight of stone spiral stairs, whose treads were worn way by the passing of generations of feet.

"I've put you and Hal on the first floor, Libby, because there is a closet close by for Harry and his nurse. Ned is at the top, and I hope you'll not mind sharing with Guy Armstrong, Ned, when he arrives. Saving those already occupied, there is scarcely another chamber in the house whose roof doesn't let in water. I'm sure you'll get on well with Guy, he is a fine man, and a great huntsman, so you'll have much in common."

Chattering on in this manner Mary led the way to the chambers. Libby was surprised, for near all Hal's family were remarkable for their taciturnity, but Libby felt sure Mary's volubility had its roots in nervousness. She could also see why Mary was, as reputed, the beauty of the family. She was very much like Hal, with the same pleasing elegance of face and figure, and the same colouring. But in Mary, the same features were cast in a feminine mould, and made lovelier still by the warmth of her smile. With comely dignity Libby found touching, Mary made them welcome to the ruinous Sidworth Castle.

Chapter Two

Once Mary departed, Libby glanced to her husband. She wondered how he'd taken Mary's outspoken words. He was silent as he looked about the chamber with its high-beamed ceiling and narrow-pointed windows. The bed looked comfortable and, Libby was relieved to see, well provided with clean, if very old, coverlets. The wind was indeed blowing at the windows and she could already feel the many draughts.

"Pray God the wind stays in the west or south," she said with a shudder. She began to take off her muddied clothes noting, with appreciation, how her maid had quickly unpacked their few garments.

Hal assented absently as he pulled an ancient chest beneath the window and climbed on it, to more properly see the view from the window, as the last of the daylight faded.

"It is not likely," he added, "it's been from the northeast most of this last week."

"Mary seems well enough," Libby remarked sighing as she tightened the laces of the bodice she would wear for supper. She thanked heaven she'd decided to bring all her really warms gowns with her on this visit.

"Yes," replied Hal quietly. "Of course, I have not seen her since her wedding near five years ago. She had miscarried and could not travel to our wedding, if you remember. However, I don't recall that she used to talk so very much, when we were children together."

"Perhaps marriage has loosened her tongue, given her confidence," suggested Libby as she studied her reflection in the spotted mirror. She wondered if her hair would frizz if she attempted to comb it. She sighed a little sigh, for she could not but compare her reflection with the face of her hostess. Libby was not a beauty, being of medium height and slender to the point of thinness. She also held herself badly, as if aware of her plain features. Her complexion was sallow. She had only once approached the dazzling beauty of Hal's sister, after being persuaded to try an application of rouge. Libby's hair was lank and, since the loss of her baby daughter some months previously, dull. Even when crimped into the riotous curls so fashionable now, it looked nothing like the lovely head of hair Mary had. Libby's smile, however, was sweet and her manner pleasing, so that once people met her, few but Libby herself ever considered her looks.

"Perhaps," Hal agreed uncertainly, "but you'll agree the letter Bess sent last month sounded most odd, and left us all feeling uneasy about Mary's state of health."

"Yes," Libby paused brushing one long ringlet about her finger, "I know Bess wrote that she felt increasing disquiet, but I didn't think Mary unstable, did you?"

"Not compared with Sir Edward's kinswoman," he replied, with a grin. "Unless it is that lady who is driving Mary to distraction. A pretty Christmas this will be with that 'death's head' at the feast!" His grin faded and he added more seriously, "My father tended to leave his daughters to the care of nurses. I was never that close to Mary, nor Jane come to that. I only know Bess well. Until now, I'd formed a different opinion of Mary's character. I had thought her more like Bess." He smiled at her doubtful reflection in the mirror. "Until then, I'd thought us something of a reserved family."

"Yes, but Ned is not particularly reserved,and no more is your father. Perhaps she more closely resembles them, than you and Bess."

"Perhaps," he agreed absently, then changing the subject added, "Is Harry settled?"

"Oh yes, Mary has set a girl to wait upon Alys and

Harry. I left him eating his supper and telling this wench of the adventures on his way here. He'll have her eating out of his hand by bed time."

"What a little rogue he is," said Hal, his voice full of proud affection. "I must say Mary seems to be making every effort in her power for our comfort."

"Although, I thought she seemed to feel it that Sir Edward wasn't here to greet us."

"Yes, but that is no great matter after all," he said magnanimously. "No doubt he was delayed by his appointment."

She nodded fastening the pearl necklace her husband had given her about her throat. "Do I look presentable, Hal?" she asked anxiously.

He came to stand behind her, smiling at her reflection in the mirror. She was a trim little body now, curled and polished, every inch a lady. He'd grown very fond of her, and was secretly proud of the ease of her transformation from an unpolished tradesman's daughter.

"Yes, you look very presentable indeed," he agreed as he bent to kiss her slender neck lightly before helping her to her feet and escorting her down to supper.

♣

The Great Hall looked welcoming once there was more candlelight. The glow thrown out by the Yule log, which was now burning merrily, gave it an almost a cosy air. The dark shadows concealed the forlorn furnishings and the faded, threadbare tapestries.

Presently, the ill-assorted company sat down and those gathered about the table were, if not exactly merry, at least affable. They were one and all seasonally inclined for good humour and the wine flowed freely.

Libby sat between Ned and Hal and was so afforded an excellent view of Sir Edward's closest neighbours, who had been bidden to share the festivity. Guy Armstrong and his sisters, Fanny, a young woman of Libby's age or older, who was of sober mien; and Cecily, a pretty lass of fifteen, who was plainly determined to extract the most enjoyment from the celebrations. Sir Edward had introduced everybody as they arrived in the Great Hall, but his manner had been curt and dismissive to the point of rudeness. It had been this, which set up Hal's hackles, as had his failure to apologise for his earlier absence. Sir Edward had not troubled to conceal his appointment had been with his pack of hounds.

Guy Armstrong was very pleasant-faced man of a similar age to Hal. He had dark mischievous eyes, a slightly pointed nose, and a neat beard. Somehow, Libby wasn't quite sure, but he reminded her of a wild creature from the forest with a slightly puckish look about him. His charm was undeniable, however, and he made it his business to be agreeable. Although he was one of the huntsmen, Guy had excused himself at once and hastened away to wash and change his clothes. He arrived back to exchange civilities with the Westwood family, once this was accomplished.

Meanwhile, Sir Edward and his kin, Walter and Geoffrey Soames, had stayed drinking the best part of a jug of wine, with their bosom companions. They made supper so late that finally Mary, with a resigned shrug, bade them sit as they were, in all their dirt, before the food was spoiled.

A burst of coarse laughter from the far end of the table made Libby glance curiously to Mistress Soames, who sat unmoved between her husband and son. Libby began to have some sympathy for her strangeness, as they leaned across her, clearly the worse for the prodigious amount of wine they'd drunk.

Libby felt very glad of Hal's protective shoulder, as their jests grew wilder. She had disliked the young man on sight, drawing back, even then, from his bold glance, hot hands and demand for a seasonal buss. For his part, Geoffrey Soames, was blessed with impressive stature, but he was also inclined to fleshiness, an impediment that his inclination to overdressed finery did little to mitigate. His eyes were too close together for her liking, and there was an unpleasant slackness about his moist mouth she found positively distasteful.

Bess, Libby knew, would find him equally unpleasant especially as she was seated next to him. Libby noticed that her usually pale skin was tinged an indignant pink, as she was forced, by good manners, to listen to his mixture of fulsome flattery and scarcely veiled innuendo, which was his manner of conversation.

"I do not think Bess finds her seat comfortable," murmured Libby into Hal's ear, as Bess shook her head sharply, in reply to her companion's words.

"No," he agreed, directing a frown the length of the table. His sister had pulled as far away from her companion as good manners would allow. Soames, who leaned across Bess's chair trapping her, seemed presently to sense Hal's cold scrutiny. He looked up and seeing Hal's unwavering stare upon him, impudently raised a wine glass in salute.

"I am sure you'll join me in a toast to Mistress Bess's beautiful eyes, Mr Westwood," he leered, with an ingratiating grin.

"I'll join you in wishing all the ladies the compliments of the season," Hal replied austerely.

"That's you slapped back into place, Geoff! " laughed Sir Edward. He was a giant of a man, rapidly going to ruin, with thin, grizzled hair, broad shoulders and sagging stomach. His face was set in grim, disagreeable lines. There was small silence. "I tell you, you'll have to mend your manners now Hal Westwood is here to teach us all how to behave!" he barked, with a curt laugh, that owed little to joviality.

Hal, well aware of the irony in Sir Edward's tone, raised his brows and said coldly, "I would not have Mr Soames alter his manners one wit for my sake; perhaps for his own?" He broke off, paused deliberately, and added with a cutting edge to his voice, "I am sure all gentlemen put the comfort of a lady foremost in mind."

"Comfort?" Sir Edward bellowed with a gust of laughter, which was not genial. "Comfort? No, 'tis conquest, not comfort, Geoff has in mind!"

"Perhaps then if he were to consider a lady's comfort first, he may find conquest follows," suggested Hal with a faintly incredulous air, which removed its affability.

"I vow, Geoff, that is paramount to an invitation to pursue your suite with the wench," cried Sir Edward. "Go to it, Geoff! After all, you have your lady's guardian's consent now."

"I am not my sister's guardian. My father is not only

alive and well, but so deep in negotiations for the hand of his daughter, as to make her a betrothed woman. As such, she should be free from the importunities of other gentlemen," snapped Hal, losing some of his calm.

"Precisely,"interrupted Guy Armstrong, judging it time to intervene."If a betrothed lady cannot be considered safe, who can, eh, Fanny?"

"Are you to be married, Mistress Armstrong?" asked Libby quietly as another burst of laughter followed the latest quip from the boisterous end of the table.

"I hope to be married in the spring, Mistress Westwood," replied the young woman, who blushed rosily and lost some of her studious air.

"My sister is betrothed to Tom Featherstone," explained Guy in an aside to Libby. "He is the rector of the village at the castle gate. He should have joined us, but was, unfortunately, called away to visit a deathbed this evening."

"Oh dear, how unfortunate," said Libby. Her glance travelled with dismay to Hal's angry face, as Geoffrey Soames continued his drunken wooing of Bess.

"Christmas is a busy time for Thomas," said Mistress Armstrong prosaically. "It is a shame he should not be here, but his flock need him, and I must learn not to complain. He does the Lord's work. We must all be happy in the knowledge we do the Lord's will."

"Indeed," echoed Libby, feeling faintly daunted by the other woman's overt saintliness.

Ned, who had been as busy eating, opened his eyes wide and wondered if Mistress Soames's malady were contagious.

Guy Armstrong's pleasant, mobile face showed his amusement at Ned's expressive countenance. "Aye, we must do our duty with a good heart," he agreed, "but some find their duty on pleasanter paths. I consider my sister a brave woman to take on a widower of slender means and seven small children, and Tom Featherstone either a fool or a hero, to take on a young woman of small dowry, however capable and good."

"Seven small children, good heavens!" gasped Libby in amazement.

"The Lord will provide, Guy. I have every confidence the Lord will provide. Has he not seen fit to provide seven motherless children with a new mother who will do her best to bring them up in the sight of His Grace?" replied Mistress Armstrong placidly.

"The elder is not ten years old and the youngest a month short of a year," said Guy Armstrong with a humorous lift of his eyebrows. "A ready-made family with a vengeance, think you not Mistress Westwood?

Cecily and I, we pray our feet will find an easier path to duty, don't we?" His younger sister flashed him a bright smile and nodded, her glance going from Hal to Ned.

"Madam, you have my congratulations," said Hal politely. "I have to tell you that my wife and I are blessed with, but the one child, as yet," he smiled faintly at Libby, "and we find him enough to handle. My respect for you has increased seven-fold."

"Better pray it doesn't increase any further, for the sake of poor Tom Featherstone and his slender purse," chuckled Guy.

"Nay, Guy, they are poor, motherless children. I will do no more for them than the next woman. And if the Lord sees fit in his wisdom to add to our brood, then he shall not provide for those children also?" replied his sister, unperturbed by his laughter.

"They are wild, unconditioned cubs for the most part, at least the boys are. And if the eldest isn't the devil incarnate, I know nothing of the matter," interjected her brother bluntly. "I am not sure if you are a saint or a fool, Fanny!"

"You are just annoyed with him because his tricks had you off your horse last week, Guy," she smiled, which immediately made her seem much more human.

Ned glanced up from where he'd been steadily eating his way through a large plate of food, and met the
laughing eyes of Cecily, who smiled at him, wrinkling
her nose in appreciation of the fun. A grin creased his
freckled face and faded slightly as his cheeks reddened.
In a moment, in that fleet second, he finally understood what all the poets had been writing about. This
sudden comprehension was followed by a feeling of
annoyance that he, too, was like other men.

"Do you hunt with us tomorrow, Mr Westwood,
indeed, both Mr Westwoods?" Guy Armstrong was
obviously following his own train of thought. "I'm not
sure if you know that Sir Edward has a stag hunt arranged for tomorrow. There is one each Christmas Eve.
Upwards of four-and-twenty staghounds and men from
all over this part of the country will be here at first
light to follow the chase. We only return at dusk."

"Ned here is the one for hunting," replied Hal wryly.
"If it moves, he'll hunt it. As for me," he sighed a little,
"my hunting days are at an end for this year, I fear. I
injured my shoulder in a fall last month and am still
not entirely fit."

"A fall out hunting?" asked Guy with ready sympathy. "Oh, bad luck!"

"Yes," replied Hal, "I've never known an autumn drag

like this one. I've been reduced to walking for exercise and all for something as stupid as a fall."

"It wasn't stupid, Hal, it was heroic," cried Libby. "You fell saving man's life!"

"Aye," cried Ned. He glanced up from his plate again, although he'd promised himself he would not. "You know, but for you riding like the wind after Jack Castleton, and catching hold of his horse after it had bolted, he'd have ridden off the edge of Coombe Down, and fallen to his death in the quarry below. He said he owed his life to you!" Ned's eyes, sparkling with admiration of his elder brother and his daring rescue, met those of the girl again, and he was pleased to see the admiration for Hal reflected in her innocent eyes.

"Aye, Ned, that same Jack Castleton also owes me a vast deal of money, which is even more to the point," said Hal, who was rather embarrassed by this praise, and so made light of it. "I am not likely to get either, and of the two, I'd rather the money."

Guy Armstrong turned to Ned midst the laughter this provoked "So, young Master Ned, you are a keen huntsman, are you?"

"Aye, when we have the time," agreed Ned temperately, though he seldom thought of anything else. "Our own country isn't of the best, but I can get a good day out with some friends, about ten miles from our home at Westwood. My sister Jane's husband, although he doesn't actually hunt, lives in superb country, so I find an excuse to visit them a few times a year."

The talk went on to become more general with this talk of the chase, as all the men joined in to discuss past glories. They told of magnificent stags, which had escaped them only by a hair's breadth; of runs after fierce boars in the lands beyond the castle; of the thick forest, where a whole pack of hounds could easily be lost; and the rolling hills, which led ever westward to the distant mountains.

Hal sat back a little and surveyed the company, pondering what he'd seen of his sister and her ungracious husband. He wondered if things really were as bad as Bess implied, or if she'd allowed her rather yielding spirits to be depressed by the dismal castle.

The meal closed in a more amicable mood, for Sir Edward went off at once with Geoffrey Soames to the stables to inspect the horses for the hunt, and the remainder of the company withdrew to the solar, a snug parlour lit by a welcoming fire, where more wine and sweetmeats were set out.

Mary, determined the conversation shouldn't be dominated by the forthcoming hunt, and tried for a topic to help weld her ill-assorted guests, recollected Hal's visit to Court the previous summer.

"Libby, you have not said; how went your visit to Whitehall? Did you see the Queen as Hal promised?"

"Indeed we did, did we not, my dear?" replied Hal as Libby nodded. "It was a wonderful, glittering occasion. We saw the Queen come down from Hampton Court by barge and the pageant on the river. There were so many vessels, one could scare see the water for them. Father pointed out the Queen, but in the press of the crowd we got a sad view."

"But what is she like, Libby?" asked Bess. "Reports say she has little beauty beside Lady Castlemaine."

"Castlemaine is a wicked whore," exclaimed Mistress Soames. "An evil woman, steeped in the sins of iniquity. There will be a judgement upon the Court of King Charles Stuart."

"The Queen is small and dark, but quite pretty, and appeared most amicable," said Libby slowly. She was in something of a quandary, for Mistress Soames's words were but an echo of her own feelings of the summer, yet the moment they fell from that lady's lips they sounded hidebound and old-fashioned. "I fear I cannot disagree with reports, Bess, the Queen lacks the great beauty of the Lady Castlemaine, but she seemed happy enough to be on the river in such fine company."

"It is said she now dresses in the English manner, is that so?" asked Mary. "One heard such tales of the perfect frights the Queen's ladies-in-waiting looked."

"Certainly their manner of dressing is different—"

"She is a Papist!" Mistress Soames had no qualms at interruptingHal. "A Papist,the same as that French woman, the King's mother, who brought our country to Civil War. How many deaths of all of our kin can be laid at her door?"

"Queen Catherine has permission to follow her own religion, I do believe," continued Hal mildly. "Indeed, I understand the King is most anxious for religious toleration throughout the land. He was gracious enough to spend some minutes talking with me on the occasion of my father receiving his knighthood."

"The Queen appears to dress exactly as we do, Mary," Libby replied. "If she were amongst us now there would be hardly any difference."

"And father, Hal, was he pleased with the honour, the occasion?" asked Mary.

"Indeed he was!" Hal grinned. "Seldom, I think, could a man have enjoyed such an occasion more."

"It is well deserved," agreed Mary, "Sir Edward was surprised it had not come earlier."

"I think our father would agree with that," Hal laughed.

"What is father's new lodging like? Where is it exactly? Oh, but I wish I could go to Court," Mary sighed enviously.

"It is an evil place, my lady," interrupted Mistress Soames. "Not a fit place for decent people. Wickedness and vice flourish at Whitehall! The King surrounds himself with lechers, fornicators and scarlet women."

"Father has taken a house just off King Street, which is a most fashionable address, I gather," said Hal, determined Mistress Soames should not stop their discussion. "Our step-mother, Jacqueline, is most pleased by all events."

As the other men fell into a discussion of the expected sport on the morrow, Libby suddenly remembered another startling piece of news. "Lady Westwood has a black serving boy called Moses. He wears a suit of red camlet with silver buttons and looks very fine in it. His skin is dark, rather like the colour of old oak, and it makes his teeth and eyes gleam white when he laughs. He runs after Lady Westwood wherever she goes and carries her muff and fan."

"A black child?" cried Mary opening her eyes wide in surprise. "Good heavens! Does he speak English?"

"Yes," Libby nodded, and then began to chuckle. "His English is as good as yours or mine, although somebody has taught him a great many oaths, which he doesn't understand the meaning of."

"Profanity is the voice of the devil," insisted Mistress Soames. "although we talk in tongues of angels without understanding—"

Hal sighed and looked up in relief as Sir Edward and Geoffrey Soames returned. They might not smell very pleasantly, and their conversation was predictably almost totally equine, but their conversation was a relief from that of Mistress Soames and, at least in their presence, she said a good deal less for the remainder of the evening.

Chapter Three

Hal awoke early next morning. He was driven from his rest by the relentless, nagging pain in his shoulder. Not wishing to disturb Libby, who slept soundly, he rose and made ready for the day with stealth. He was glumly aware that it would be a long one, with the most of the men out hunting, but unable to see any help for it. Unless the leaden skies improved, allowing him the chance of a little exercise on foot, he was condemned to spend the day indoors.

He came down the spiral stairs of the tower in the same light-footed manner, shivering slightly. The wind, as predicted, had turned to the northeast, and a faint smell of smoking chimneys pervaded the air.

At the base of the stair, he paused to stare in astonishment at the sight of his sister, Mary, standing in the doorway, of what appeared to be her bedchamber, embracing Guy Armstrong. Hal stood for a moment or two in the shadows, a feeling of stupefaction creeping over him. Mary, whom he had previously looked upon as the model of a good and faithful wife, was in the arms of her neighbour and, what was more, plainly enjoying his attention. Anger rose up in him as, he realised, she was still in her night attire and the implications of this sank in. That any sister of his could so far forget herself as to encourage the advances of a man seemed almost beyond belief. Without giving himself time to consider the matter further, he stepped forward into the dim gallery, a determined look in his eye.

The lovers fell apart, as if at the sound of his step. Guy Armstrong caught up his heavy cloak and hurried off toward the main stairs and the hunting party. Mary, having thrown a kiss after his retreating figure, silently closed her door on the sleeping house.

Hal filled with righteous indignation, bounded across the wide gallery, barely pausing outside the door before rapping lightly on the polished oak. It opened at once to show Mary, her eyes, soft and dreamy, a smile playing about her lips. This faded abruptly at the sight of her brother's flinty face. "Where can we talk privately?" he demanded, in a harsh whisper.

"My chamber?" she replied indicating the room behind her.

"Your husband, is he still not abed?" he demanded.

"No, he—he has another chamber. He will have arisen already at this hour for the hunt. We do not—it—it is many months since we last shared a bed," she stammered, and stood back, allowing him to enter her large, panelled chamber. The tumbled tester-bed bore mute witness to the fact that more than one had occupied it. This sight made him feel even angrier.

"Why is that?" he demanded. "I was under the impression it was to secure an heir, that Sir Edward married you."

Mary blushed and walked to pick up a bed-gown. She occupied herself with securing it about her slender waist. "So he professed at our wedding," she replied quietly, "but now he claims my failure to produce the required heir within these last two years is evidence I am barren. He refuses to waste any more of his valuable time on me, and you find me banished here." Her voice, in spite of her efforts to appear at ease, was strained and clogged with unshed tears.

Hal felt a wave of compassion for her disappointed hopes, but thrust them aside as he recollected the scene witnessed a few moments earlier. "And so you seek to find comfort in the arms of another?" he snapped.

"Comfort? No!" she protested.

"No? Yet I've just seen you!" he cried angrily. "I saw you with my own eyes, locked in that fellow Armstrong's embrace. You little fool! Don't you see the danger which threatens you?"

She turned to face him, her cheeks pale now, "I love him," she said simply.

"Stuff and nonsense!" he replied roundly. "You are a married woman."

"A married woman," she repeated with a hollow laugh, which verged on a note of hysteria. "Aye, I'm married indeed. Married to a drunken pig of a man, who uses me ill."

Hal's eyes narrowed, and he glanced at her, as if to measure the truth of her words. "What mean you?" he demanded.

She turned from him again, unable to bear his scrutiny. "Oh, how can I hope to explain?" she cried. "There's never any point. You are happily married. You love Libby. You can have no conception of how it is to be forced to endure the advances of a man who repels one physically."

Hal crossed to the window where she stood. The curtain had been pulled back to reveal the dour landscape. He touched her arm softly. "Yes, I do have a great affection for Libby," he agreed in more gentle tones, "but I was not, in love, as the saying goes, when we were married. I can understand your feeling, to a certain degree. There is certain distaste in the cold-blooded manner of being forced to share intimate moments with what is, in effect, a complete stranger. But the strangeness passes, Mary. A duty, even a disagreeable one, faced up to, accomplished, soon becomes a duty no more. As time passes, affection can grow."

"Forgive me, but—affection grow?" she cried wildly, interrupting him. "Oh, Hal, you have no idea of what you are talking about!" She caught his hand as he drew back offended, for it had cost him something to speak out as he had. "Oh, no, don't, please, I am sorry. I know you mean well. I'd not expected you to be so very kind, but Hal, you still don't understand."

He looked into her distraught face, seeing how she trembled, and tears welled in her great hazel eyes. "Make me understand then," he replied simply. "Tell me."

She bit at her plump bottom lip, releasing his hand. "Where to begin?" she asked almost to herself. "How to start such a sorry tale?"

"At the beginning?" He glanced about the chamber and seeing a chest against the far wall, crossed to sit on it. "Come, sit beside me and try to tell me. Believe me, when I say that I do understand what a woman feels on her marriage, for Libby has told me of her feelings."

A faint smile crossed her face at this confession. Pausing to cast a small log on the embers of the fire flickering in the hearth, she came to join him. "I am so glad you and Libby are happy, Hal," she said wistfully. "It gives the rest of us hope." She sighed as she sat down at his side, the smile fading, to leave her face strained. "You'll well remember, Hal, how I was married the summer before you," she began quietly. "Oliver Cromwell had just died and his son, Richard, taken his place. You'll remember how we, of the King's party, despaired. It seemed we would never be allowed to go home to England. Well, I was Father's attempt to get back. Sir Edward had connections in Parliament, and he promised Father he could obtain a free pardon as part of the marriage settlement. A promise he promptly failed to redeem," she hesitated, blushing again. "I was nineteen, Hal, and had been brought up with little idea of the world. You say Libby has told you something of what a woman feels in her marriage to a total stranger, but at least her bridegroom was both young and handsome. Sir Edward was, even then, an old man."

There was silence for a few moments, as the fire began to draw through and Hal reflected upon her words. She continued quietly, "I make no complaint of that.

No doubt, I endured no more than many a bride in a mis-matched marriage. It is the way of the world, so they say. Indeed, Lady Penhaligan, Sir Edward's cousin, congratulated me that I'd not be forced to endure the selfish fumbling of an inexperienced younger man!" She laughed again and the note of hysteria was present as she shuddered. "You spoke of duty, Hal. Yes, I was instructed as to my duty on that occasion, and I clung to it—and the belief that by doing that duty—I was improving the fortunes of my family. That made it endurable—just! But, there is a difference you see, I didn't know at first. How could I hope to, innocent that I was? Sir Edward has odd preferences—he—he—likes one to fear him, you see."

"Fear him?" repeated Hal frowning.

"Yes, fear," she replied and her embarrassment was even more marked. "Women, servants, dogs, horses, all must fear him. Not just a little, but hold him in dread. Each must be cowed by him. Walk in terror of his coming. Tremble with horror in his presence."

"I have not observed you to do so," he said quickly, as she shut her eyes to ward off her fears.

"No, not now," she agreed. "With terror—abject terror—either one surrenders and is destroyed, or overcomes it and is saved."

He frowned thoughtfully at this. "I don't under-stand," he said bluntly. "How did he terrify you?"

"At first, by his personality, then with threats, and finally with violence."

"Violence?" he asked sharply.

"Yes, violence—and beatings, endless beatings," she replied, and her voice seemed drained of all emotion. "He'd lock me in a chamber, refuse me all food and drink, and beat me day after day after day."

"By heaven, Mary! Why did you never say?" he cried, horrified. "Why did you never write and say so?"

"Because he wouldn't allow it," she replied wearily. "He reads all my correspondence—or he used to. He tore up any which suggested I was not perfectly happy, beating me all the more. Don't you understand? I was totally in his power."

Hal looked confounded, but this emotion was ousted by rising anger. Part against himself, that his sister should have suffered; part against his father, for not bothering about the personality of the man he wed his daughter to; and yet more against the man himself.

"How did you escape this power?" he asked grimly.

"To live like that, in constant terror," she explained, with a weary sigh. "It appears something happens in the mind. It becomes dulled. There is no hope, and so after a time, one gives up the will to live, can fight no more. I—I retreated into myself," she paused, her voice shaking, "I believe I even became a little mad, I don't know. All I do know is that, once I was destroyed, once I became a hollow wreck of myself, wild-eyed and scurrying into corners, he lost interest in me. He said I was of no use to him. I was mad and stupid—and even barren. Then he—he just seemed to forget my existence." She shrugged her shoulders. "For a while, six months or so, I was content. All I wanted was to live without fear of him. I avoided all sight of him, scuttling from his presence like a mouse, whenever I could. Then, back in the summer I met Guy." Her eyes, which had been those of a lost, tormented soul, brightened. "It was Guy who brought me back from the edge of despair. His gentleness, his love and affection, has made me want to live again."

"Aye, I can see that," he said gently, "and I give thanks for it, but there is no future for you, Mary. For, in spite of all, you are still married to Sir Edward."

"I do not care," she replied placidly. "You don't understand, but then you'd have to have sunk to the depths of despair, as I did, then you'd see. Just to be alive, to know Guy loves me, is enough. Anyway, Sir Edward is an old man. He may die at any time."

"Aye, and he may live another twenty years," replied Hal curtly. "What then? Armstrong can't wait twenty years for you to be free."

"He says we will," she replied with a smile. "Or perhaps, Sir Edward might consider divorcing me. He still needs an heir."

"Aye," he replied grimly, "and might yet be supplied with one, care of Master Armstrong! Oh Mary, take care," he cried, as she suddenly turned her face from him. "By heaven, only think of the furore he'd raise if he were to find out!"

She turned back to him, blushing rosily. "I care not," she said defiantly. "I'd be honoured to bear a child for Guy. Don't you see? We truly love each other and that is a splendid, fine thing."

"An adulterous liaison is an adulterous liaison, regardless of the fine feelings of love you and your paramour have for each other!" he said harshly. "Well enough, I suppose, if it can be kept secret. Although, to my mind, you are still betraying your marriage vows. The trouble is, these things never are kept secret for long."

"No!" She pushed away his harsh words of condemnation. "I betray nothing, for my marriage was nothing. A few words mumbled by a minister that binds me to a monster, who neither likes, nor cares for me? That marriage ended months ago, when he left me a cowering, weeping wreck on my chamber floor. I have since given my pledge to Guy and consider myself betrothed to him."

"As a married woman you have no right to give a pledge to any, but your husband." Hal was getting angrier. "You don't know how sorry it makes me, Mary, that you should have to endure this dreadful marriage. I'll speak to Sir Edward before we leave and make him understand that I will not countenance him offering you violence. That, if he should do so again, I will incite the majesty of law upon him. But, regardless of these circumstances, you are married 'til death do you part. So, you must renounce this affair with Guy Armstrong, for it greatly weakens your position as a wronged wife."

"Weakens my position?" she cried, laughing. "What position? Oh Hal, you haven't understood at all! Guy is the only reason I have for living. I will not give up my love for him. I'd sooner give up my life!"

"Now you are being foolish," he snapped sharply. "My dear, I understand you have endured a great deal, but you must look at this sensibly. You are married to Sir Edward. Your duty must be to him."

She turned to him, meeting his eyes defiantly. "Don't dare talk to me of duty, Hal!" she cried. "I've done my duty, and much good it did us. I was sacrificed for a few months political advantage for father. My life became a living hell, that father might get the chance to return from exile. No, Hal, I'm afraid I've done as much duty as I am prepared to do. In future, I look out for me. Father can take his chances elsewhere."

"It seems to me, you are forgetting your obligations to him as easily as you've abandoned them to your husband," said Hal austerely.

"Obligations? For fathering me into this uncertain world, and promptly forgetting about me for the next nineteen years?" she cried in mounting anger. "Oh, aye, he fed and clothed us, after a fashion. And, depending on how plump his purse was, supplied us with a procession of nurses, but I don't recall him ever directly speaking to any of us as children. No, Hal, each one of us, as we came of an age to be useful, were nothing but pawns to be used in his games of ambition. Each one to be sacrificed for some new advantage!"

"I do not see it so," he snapped coldly.

"No, but then I forget it was different for you. You were his son and heir, and yet even you he sold to Uncle Henry. Of course, Uncle Henry was a better man and he, at least, had the arranging of your marriage. But what, Hal, if Uncle Henry hadn't chosen Libby? What if he'd allied you to a squint-eyed spinster of uncertain years, or a feeble-minded simpleton? Tell me, if that had been the case, would you be quite so righteous?"

"How can I say?" he replied curtly, recollecting these had, indeed, been his fears before he'd met Libby. "I only know, I'd have done my duty."

"Aye, and it's easy enough to prate of duty if it's pleasant," she snapped, "but think of me, tied to an evil, drunken old man. Think of Jane with Philip Eustace. He is nothing but a vicious, spoilt boy. You do know what is said of him, don't you?"

"I've heard like you, no doubt, malicious rumours, probably much exaggerated," he said testily.

"Do you truly believe so?" she countered, meeting his eyes again. "Truly? And now here is Bess, to be the next sacrifice. Bess, who was promised a love match with Libby's brother, to be allied to Jack Petherbridge."

"A brilliant match," interrupted Hal sharply. "His father is a very wealthy man, and Bess will want for nothing!"

"Indeed no, especially not the pox," retorted Mary. "For he is reputed a libertine at a Court, which is notorious for its rakes. He is known to have a string of mistresses and regularly haunt the stews of Southwark! His conduct is a byword for all this is wicked. Yet Bess, sweet gentle Bess, is to be wed to him. How will she fare with such a man?"

"He has indicated, or at least his father, Sir William, has indicated, that Jack is wishful to put aside the follies of his youth and contract a suitable alliance," said Hal, in his stuffiest manner. "You may be assured, Mary, that father has our best interests at heart, in all the alliances he makes for his children."

"That just isn't true, Hal," she insisted quietly. "The sooner you force yourself to admit it, the better for us all. Why must you try so desperately to make a hero of father? Why won't you admit he is little better than an adventurer, who would, and for all we know, did, sacrifice his own mother to his advantage?"

"Because I have a sense of honour and duty," he replied in outraged tones.

"No, because you fear to look the truth in the face," she responded sharply. "Because you lack the courage, Hal, to stand up against him and at least see Bess made happy."

"You know nothing of the matter," he cried, stung.

"On the contrary, I know everything of it, for I have endured what waits for Bess and I am no longer afraid!"

Having no reply to this, Hal got to his feet, anger at her jibes seething in him yet, as ever, kept rigorously under control. "I shall discuss the matter of your ill-treatment with Sir Edward at the earliest opportunity," he said with cold formality.

"What, Hal, nothing more to say, so you run away?" she taunted. "No, do not trouble yourself. I am used to fighting my own battles."

"It is no trouble. It is my duty," he replied, walking to the door.

"And you'll be wasting your time," retorted Mary as he went out. "I'll not waste my time," she added to herself, "for I am determined upon my course."

Chapter Four

Prey to great irritation, Hal left his sister. Marriage, it seemed, had greatly changed her. He realised, with further annoyance, that her mere year's seniority had given her a lecturing tone in her dealings with him, which, after the deference of Libby and Bess, jarred on his sensitivities.

Hal joined the hunting party in the Great Hall, who were partaking of a substantial, and in some cases, entirely liquid, breakfast. He had been hoping for the chance of speaking to Guy Armstrong, but never got the opportunity in the general melee. Instead, he stood talking to Ned and another neighbour, until the sound of the horn called all from the tables.

Then, he followed the hunters out into the courtyard, standing back to enjoy the spectacle of the hunt. The horses' hooves clattering on the cobblestones; the yapping and snarling of the dogs as they circled each other; the bonhomie of the huntsmen as they made ready for the day; The air was frosty, the wind biting; Already noses were red, and eyes streaming. Another call from the horn, and they started away; those on foot, running with the hounds; the riders following after, still laughing and talking. Hal longed to mount up and go with them, and as the last of hunters passed through the gateway, he felt a keen recollection of being left behind as a child, when his father rode off. Giving himself a shake, as the wind gusted around the yard, he turned back to the house. He had many hours to while away, so he decided to go on a tour of the ramshackle castle.

For those remaining behind, the day started rather more slowly. The women, once they'd broken their fast, set about the numerous tasks attendant on the season. Each was well aware that, at some point near dusk, a contingent of hungry men would descend upon the castle. Much of the early part of the day was spent in preparing for this event, and the feast on the following day.

A little after noon, Bess found time to walk to the gatehouse on an errand for her sister and was amazed to hear her name called. Looking like a startled fawn, she hurried through the entrance of the gatehouse in pursuit of the call. She peered through the sleety rain and cast a doubtful glance at the lowering sky, before noticing the figure concealed alongside the bridge over the moat.

"Justin? Oh, Justin!" In a second she was in his arms, her amazed eyes raised to his face, never giving another thought to the worsening weather.

"Oh, my love, my love," he murmured into her silky hair, holding her tightly. "It has been so long!"

"It's seemed a lifetime, Justin," she gasped, resting her head against his chest and struggling to hold back the tears.

"More than six months," he replied, hugging her to him, as if he'd never let her go. "The longest six months of my life."

"I know, I know," she whispered, tears beginning to fall. "But it —it is hopeless, Justin, hopeless. Hal has done his utmost for us, I know he has. He wrote to London once again last month and begged father to reconsider. He pleaded our cause to the best of his ability, but father is adamant. I must make a better match than a country lawyer."

"My own father is now equally against the match," sighed Justin. "It seems they are determined to keep us apart."

"My father had given us his word that we could be

married," Bess despaired quietly. "I cannot believe he would go back on it, as he has. Not after he promised we might be wed."

"That was after we'd just cleared his name of murder," said Justin bitterly. "Since that date he has become more important in the eyes of the world. And my father has seen fit to haggle over your dowry."

"Did you know Hal has offered to make up the sum your father named?" she asked, raising tear-drenched eyes to his.

"No, I did not," he replied, unable to withstand the desire to kiss the tip of her pretty nose. "That was good of him. He has made no mention of it, but then we've not spoken since September when, I am afraid, we parted with coldness."

"Yes, I know, Libby told me of the quarrel over my dowry in her letter," said Bess. "It still preys on her mind that you are on bad terms, poor dear, and she is not bearing this new baby easily either."

"What? Is she with child again?" he asked anxiously. "Oh, that's splendid news! She was so heartbroken at the death of her baby last summer."

"Yes," replied Bess, looking troubled. "It was that which decided me I must leave Westwood for a while and come here. I could see Libby was pining to see you more often, and, once father had forbidden our meetings, it became so difficult for her to see you. Yet, even now, it doesn't seem to have answered, does it? For you don't visit Libby at Westwood since the quarrel."

"No," he agreed with a small sigh. "I only visit when I know Hal won't be there, and since his accident he's been tied by the heels. I can't deny the situation has often caused difficulties for us."

"Yes," she nodded, "I know we shouldn't even think of meeting like this, Justin, but, oh, I had to agree to Mary's suggestion, just this once. You see—," she continued as tears spilt over, "you see, my father has found me another husband and written to say he'll sign contracts for my marriage just after Twelfth Night. This must be goodbye."

Justin's thin face went even paler. "I had been expecting something like this," he said, his voice trembling with suppressed emotion. "As far as your father is concerned, it is the only certain way to end this matter."

She nodded again hopelessly, adding in choked accents, "I told him when we last met, I'd not marry any but you, but he merely threatened to beat me, and cast me out if I did not obey him." She raised her eyes to his face again. "It would not be so hard to bear perhaps, if my intended husband were a man of character I could respect, but Hal says he is a libertine and a gambler."

"A libertine?" cried Justin in dismay. "What is your father thinking of?"

"Jack Petherbridge is the son of a viscount," she explained tearfully. "In the eyes of the world it is a splendid match. Hal says we've done all we can do, and I must accept what I cannot change. But I can't, Justin, I cannot. I cannot bring myself to destroy all our hopes and dreams of happiness and be the dutiful daughter my father requires."

"When your father suggests you match with a rake, I say the time for obedience is past," he cried angrily. "I'd not want to lead you astray, Bess. If you feel you cannot stand matters as they are, if it would be easier for you to do as Hal advises, and give way to your father's demands, then you have but to say so. I'll not level a word of reproach at you, but if you are, indeed, determined not to marry this man, or any other, then there are steps we can take, if only we are bold enough."

"Steps?" she asked, shivering as the icy wind gusted past them.

He took off his heavy cloak and put it around her tenderly. "In short, we could be married clandestinely."

"In secret?" she gasped, opening her eyes wide in amazement.

"Aye," he replied, holding her gaze intently.

"But how? Why? What use would that be?" she asked puzzled. "I don't want to be married in secret. I want everyone to know."

"Hush," he soothed, "if we were married secretly, then you could not be forced to marry another. Or at least, if you were to be forced, the second marriage would not be legal."

"But is a secret marriage legal? How could it be accomplished?" she asked in amazement.

"Under common law it is legal, provided—" he hesitated, "provided the marriage has been consummated."

"Consume— oh," she blushed, "oh, I see, yes."

"And we'd need two witnesses of good character, too," he continued.

"Witnesses? To—to the consummation?" she cried in horror.

"No, no," he laughed softly, squeezing her frozen hands. "We need witnesses only to the fact that we have spent the night together, in each other's company." He paused scanning her pale face, his glance measuring. "I can't deny it's a big step to take, Bess. And, like you, when your sister Mary suggested it in her letter, I was taken aback. I saw all too clearly as you do, the disad-vantages. You have much to lose. Your good name, your father's—nay your family's, approval. Then, I realised Mary would stand by you, and I began to consider it more and more. And then, so enamoured did I become of the plan, I obtained a bishop's licence and brought it with me, just as Mary said I should."

"You have a licence?" she asked, a ray of hope dawn-ing on her face. "Oh, Justin, then if we are bold enough, we could be certain, in the end, to be together?"

He grimaced. "Not necessarily. If the worst came to worst, it would mean we could never be married to another. At least, not until after your father's demise, which might be many years hence. Even after that, Hal may feel obliged to continue the objections. I want you to understand this, Bess. It could well be we will never be allowed to live together as man and wife, because we'll both be disowned. The only way is if you consent to live with me as a pauper."

"I'd care nothing for that," she cried hugging him. "Would you?"

"For myself, no," he agreed. "Though I think it might gall me if I had to see my wife and children starve for want of money, when I should have had a comfortable inheritance."

"But your father wouldn't disown you, Justin," she said softly, "he adores you."

"That's as may be, but he will not be best pleased if you come dowerless, my love," he replied factually.

"You think he might refuse his consent, if I have no dowery?" Her face fell. "Of course he would, how foolish of me. I don't think I could bear it either, if you had to spend your days toiling as a miserable clerk, to keep your family housed and fed. Oh, Justin, what should we do for the best?"

"That is something you must decide, my darling." He kissed the tip of her nose again. "I have had time to think, time to consider all aspects. I know what I want." He paused and then added slowly, "One more thing, Bess. Bear in mind that if you should decide to go ahead with this scheme, which, as a sober-minded lawyer, I must condemn as madness, you may have to consider never being a mother, never bearing children. It is in the power of our parents to send us away and part us entirely for the rest of our lives."

"Yes," she glanced up at him, and seeing how serious his face was, experienced a moment of doubt. "What do you want to do, Justin?"

"You know what I want, Bess," he replied, holding her eyes in a manner which made her senses swim, "I want you. Whatever the cost to us both, whatever the pain and suffering, I want you as my wife. I want us to be married."

"So do I want that, Justin," she replied. "So do I!"

"No, my love, no!" He pressed her hands to his chest, hugging them. "No, I want you to think about it, reflect on it. I am here until Twelfth Night, unless Hal objects so strongly as to send me away! I want you to think about it and let me know what you decide."

He smiled faintly. "I am tempted to say your answer would make the most wonderful Christmas gift, but I'll press you no more." He darted a glance over his shoulder as voices were heard in the courtyard beyond. "We must part, my darling, and I doubt we'll be allowed to spend much time together, but be sure I'll be thinking of you always!" He held her close for a few seconds, and then stepped out of the shadow of the gatehouse to look into the yard, beckoning to her when he saw the coast was clear. They embraced briefly once more, then she surrendered his cloak, and darted away into the house.

Justin donned his cloak again in a leisurely manner, walked back several yards to retrieve his horse and baggage. Then, after a short space of time, rode under the archway and into the courtyard.

He handed his weary mount to one servant, and followed another into the house, where a third was waiting to take his name. Justin glanced about him with a rueful expression as he bent to warm his hands at the fire, wondering what the next few days would bring.

Chapter Five

Hal spent the morning on a tour of Sidworth Castle. It was not an experience he enjoyed. In the months since his uncle's death he and Ned had worked hard on their home, the Westwood estate. They were young and untried, and, Hal was sure, they often made mistakes, but for all their failures, and there had been a few, Westwood Hall stood in good heart.

This was not the case at Sidworth Castle. If it had been Hal's estate he would have felt nothing but shame, and would never have allowed himself a day's rest until some order had been created from the muddle all about him. His opinion of Sir Edward Jolyon was not improved.

His investigations had, however, determined the location of Sir Edward's library. It was in a small, dark closet off the gallery and, judging from the antiquity and dusty appearance of the books, they were the possessions of one of Sir Edward's ancestors. Hal selected a book and decided that, even with the candle, it would be impossible to read in the closet, so he came back down the staircase.

At the foot of the stairs, he noticed a tall stranger standing before the smoking fire. He was surprised a neighbour would choose this time to call, when the whole countryside was out hunting with Sir Edward.

"May I be of help?" he asked politely. Hal was aware, even as he spoke, of something familiar about the man, but was unable to see his face in the dim December afternoon. "Sir Edward is, I fear, from home. My sister, his wife must be at—"

"Hal!" cried Justin as he spun about to face him in dismay, for Hal was the very last person he hoped to meet this side of suppertime.

"You?" said Hal blankly. "What do you here? Your father—he is not ill—dead?" he added, unable to think of any another explanation.

"No, I thank you. He is both alive and well, and is spending the feast with his cousin Dorothy in Chawcester, as is our custom," Justin replied in astonishment.

"Oh, thank heaven," cried Hal, in heartfelt accents. "I beg pardon, but the idea suddenly flashed into my head. Such a thing would have broken Libby's heart, aye, and probably cost her the unborn baby."

"My father is perfectly well, I assure you," said Justin warmly, pleased to see Hal's concern for his wife. "So Libby is to have another child? I congratulate you, and wish her well. I trust she is fully recovered by now, from the tragic death of her baby daughter?"

"Yes," said Hal shortly, then clammed up as he always did when the death of their last child was mentioned. "Yes, thank you."

An uncomfortable silence followed, both recollecting how they had parted with coolness three months earlier. Then Hal said, with some awkwardness, "I fear Libby is abed resting at present, but my sister Mary must be about the house somewhere. You are expected?"

Justin, who had foreseen the question, replied coolly, "Lady Jolyon has been kind enough to extend an invitation for me to pass the Christmastide here at Sidworth Castle."

"Oh, has she?" replied Hal, a grim tone entering his voice, as he guessed what his sister was up to.

"Yes, Lady Jolyon knows, of course, I'd not had the opportunity of seeing Libby much of late, and so, was good enough to invite me," Justin added, recollecting on the phrases Mary had employed in her letter.

"How kind of her," replied Hal, with a sarcastic tone.

"Tell me, for how long have you had the pleasure of Lady Jolyon's acquaintance?"

"I have not yet, in fact, met Lady Jolyon," he replied with an attempt at the urbane. "However, I am hoping you'll be able to remedy the matter presently, by introducing her to me."

"This is intolerable," cried Hal, his annoyance getting the better of him. "I cannot believe that even Mary would connive at such a trick."

"You cannot believe I'd what, Hal? Oh, you must be Mr Danvers," Mary said, as she came from behind the screens at the opposite end of the hall, her arms full of greenery. She took in the scene with but one glance at Hal's wrath-filled face. "Bess! Bring those ribbons and come to greet Libby's brother. Have you seen Libby, Mr Danvers? No, of course you won't, for is she not resting in her chamber? But Hal, as your brother-in-law will have been looking after you. Hal, have you not called for mulled wine for our guest?"

"No, I have not, Mary. And I tell you, this will not do!" he cried angrily as Bess, looking rather apprehensive, but unable to conceal her delight, hastened into the hall in her sister's wake, carrying a posy of brightly coloured ribbons.

"May I not take that holly from you, ma'am?" Justin

asked as he came to relieve Mary of her heavy basket.

"Oh, thank you, sir," she paused to shake hands firmly with him, looking him in the face as she said, "I am pleased to finally make your acquaintance, Mr Danvers. It is so nice to welcome yet another of my family to Sidworth Castle."

"Mary, I say, this will not do," repeated Hal, raising his voice, seeing she paid him no heed.

"But it will, Hal, I assure you," she replied imperturbably. "Done up with ribbons and hung about the hall, it will serve very well. Even though there are precious few berries on the holly this year. Ah, Meg, is that you at last? Bring flagons of mulled wine, and some goblets, and be quick about it, girl."

"I will be heard!" Hal, white with fury at her total disregard for what he was saying, raised his voice even more. "I cannot, nay will not, stand by and allow this outrage!"

"Outrage?" Mary came to stand calmly before him. "Where is the outrage?"

"You, in inviting Justin Danvers here. It is well known he and Bess are forbidden to meet. You know they are not to be married. Don't you see this makes everything doubly hard?"

Furiously, he rounded on his brother-in-law, "And

you, Justin, I'd have thought you too much of a man of honour to come here to distress and embarrass my sister."

"I, a man of honour?" returned Justin, his eyes glittering disdainfully. "I thought I was little better than a tradesman. Or so you said, on the last occasion of our meeting. That being the case, and no longer having to sustain the character of a gentlemen, a feat clearly beyond me, I decided to consult my own pleasure." His face softened as he glanced to Bess. "It was my pleasure to spend Christmastide with the two women most dear to me."

"This is impossible," said Hal, although he spoke with less heat now, as Bess blushed prettily and returned the glowing look Justin cast upon her. "I must insist you leave at once, Danvers."

"At once? At this time of day, with the weather worsening, and snow expected?" asked Mary. "Do not be a fool, Hal! Besides which, is Justin to be banished without even bidding his sister the season's compliments? I don't think she'd thank you for that."

"No good can come of this," cried Hal as he began to get angry again, especially at the thought of how upset and disappointed Libby was going to be. "Don't you see? This will cause more misery." He glanced from one hostile, defiant face to another, adding, "I cannot force you to leave, of course, Justin. This is not my house, but I can forbid Bess to speak to you."

"You would not be so cruel!" cried Mary, shocked to see him so inflexible.

"Or better still, demand your word of honour that you'll make no attempt to speak to her. For I must warn you, sir," continued Hal, very much in the grand manner, "my sister is a betrothed woman."

"No, I am not betrothed, Hal," insisted Bess, clearly and quietly, although she blushed hotly and shook with emotion. "I have not given my consent to the match our father proposes. And I shall never give my consent to any proposal, save one from Justin."

Justin's eyes flew to her face, as he wondered if this was her answer.

Then, as Hal exclaimed in wrath, Libby entered the hall, leading her small son by the hand. "See here, Harry, here is the greenery all gathered. Oh, Justin!" Letting go of the child's hand abruptly, she ran the length of the hall and into her brother's arms, tears of joy running down her face. "Oh, Justin, Justin, what a surprise!"

Hal experienced a stab of pure jealousy and was instantly ashamed of himself. He wondered if it was that, as much as fear of Bess eloping with Justin, that had made him ban his brother-in-law from Westwood. Pushing the thought from his mind, he took a firm grip of his temper and crossed the dim hall to pick up his son, Harry, lifted the bewildered child into his arms, and returned to the group at the fireside.

"Justin!" Libby was still exclaiming. "What do you here? I never expect—what do you here?"

"Why, I invited your brother, Libby," replied Mary as she met her own brother's steely gaze defiantly. "I knew you'd be more than happy to see Justin—Bess, too!"

"Oh, Bess, but Hal—," Libby turned to her husband with guilt and consternation on her face. She was aware he'd be furiously angry by the turn of events.

"It is the season of goodwill and peace," interrupted Mary. "Even Hal must allow a little leeway over Christmastide. Good heavens, as if Hal would behave in a truly medieval manner, and demand that Bess and Justin have no communication whatsoever."

Libby laughed weakly, as everyone held their collective breath. Hal, out-manoeuvred, firmly closed his lips over a hasty retort, and directed a look at his brazen sister, which spoke volumes.

"Oh, Justin, I am so glad to see you," said Libby softly, as she embraced him yet again. "I have missed you so."

"I've missed you, too," he agreed, but with half an eye on Hal's thunderous countenance. "Tell me, are you quite well now? I did not know you were to have another child. When is it due? Have you told father yet?"

"No, for he worries so and there is ample time before it is born in the spring," she replied. She sat down on the chair he drew forward for her, taking the goblet of mulled wine Mary handed her. Hal released his wriggling son and watched him stagger across to help Bess and her tangle of ribbons, whilst trying to hear what his wife and brother-in-law were discussing in low-toned voices.

"Wine, Hal?" asked Mary, meeting the challenge in his eyes.

"Thank you," he replied curtly and having taken a sip he abandoned his fruitless eavesdropping. He put the wine aside and crossed the hall to pick up several of the branches of holly, which he held out for Bess to bind up with bright red ribbons.

"Wine for you, Bess?" Mary hastened to her side, to assist in her defence.

"No, thank you," she returned lowly, adding under her breath, "Until today, Hal, I had no idea of it. I swear to you!"

Hal met her eyes, his own grim. "Possibly not," he conceded grudgingly. "It seems I'll be an ogre if I demand, as I should, that Justin is less to you than a stranger."

Bess gently took a ribbon from Harry, who was sucking the end of it and tied a sadly lopsided bow on the branches Hal held out to her. "I'll obey you if you command me to ignore him, Hal," she replied, fighting to keep back tears.

"You put me in an intolerable situation—you and Mary," he cried, his anger flaring again at the sound of unhappiness in her voice. "You both know right from wrong. I am not the keeper of your consciences. You must do as you see fit. Don't expect me to approve your defiance."

She bit her lip and tears spilled over at his harshness, trickling down her face and staining the gay ribbon in her hands. "Oh, Hal, I do love Justin so!"

Hal angrily broke a too long branch, jarring his shoulder painfully. He thought, with equal pain, of how he hated this role his father had thrust upon him. He knew Bess and Justin loved each other deeply and that his father had promised Justin her hand in marriage. Yet, his father's change of mind meant he must stand out against them all. He must wound Justin, as good a fellow as he was; hurt Bess, his best-loved sister; disappoint his wife; and widen the rift between himself and Mary.

"You know, Bess, it is our duty to obey father in all things," he said, his voice stern.

"Yes," she replied hopelessly, tears coursing down her cheeks.

"Oh, goddamn it," he cried, his heart melting at her despair. "Don't weep so. For the love of Christ, don't weep, girl. You know I cannot bear to see you weep! Speak to him, if you must. Love him, if you will. For this Christmastide, at least, we'll call a truce."

"Oh, Hal, may we?" cried Libby running to join him, as Justin came to comfort Bess. "May we not forget all these horrid quarrels and be like we once were before, one big, happy family?"

His arm came about her thickening waist and he hugged her to him briefly. "Mary tells me it is the season of peace and goodwill to all men, even to your brother Justin." He smiled wryly at his grave brother-in-law, as he glanced up from soothing Bess. "Pax?" he suggested, half in jest, offering his hand.

Justin hesitated for a split second, then reached forward to take it. "Peace," he agreed, but there was a note of reservation in his voice.

Hal might not have been quite so at peace with the world in general if he'd been privy to a conversation later that evening before supper. Mary conducted her latest guest to his chamber personally, as was her custom.

"Well, Mr Danvers, now we are finally out of earshot, I can ask you the question I have been longing to, this hour past. Is everything in train?"

"I have procured a licence as you suggested, ma'am," he replied frowning a little.

"Excellent, I knew you would not fail!" she exclaimed. "So there is nothing to stop us. Famous! Now, I have arranged everything as I wrote to you I would, for to-night so—"

"For tonight?" he cried, startled.

"Yes," she replied glancing at him. "Why, is ought amiss? Do you have second thoughts, sir? Are you no longer willing?"

"I? Indeed, no!" he cried. "But earlier today, I told Bess to consider the matter carefully. It is not possible for the ceremony to go forward tonight. She has not had enough time to consider all the aspects of the case."

"But it must," said Mary blankly, "Mr Featherstone, the rector, can only be here this evening. Thereafter he'll be busy with services in the village church, so it must be tonight, or you must wait until after Christmas."

"Then we must wait until after, ma'am," he replied sharply, "for I'll not have Bess hurried into a decision."

"You'll not have Bess at all, if you don't have a care," she replied tartly. "Have you not understood? The contracts for her marriage to Jack Petherbridge are to be signed by Twelfth Night, so it is likely my father will send for Bess immediately after St. Stephen's Day. For undoubtedly, she should be present at the signing of the contract."

He stared fixedly at her. "No, I had not thought of that, fool that I am," he replied honestly. "Yet what to do? For hurry Bess into a decision, I will not."

"You should never have given Bess a decision at all," said Mary crossly. "She is a dear, sweet girl, but decisiveness is not in her nature. She will vacillate for days, if something is not done. You'd best seek her out again and tell her you must—and shall—be married this evening."

"I shall do no such thing!" he cried horrified. "I would not so insult the woman I love!"

She glanced to him, her smile wry. "Yes, you are very young," she said, with all the wisdom of one five years the elder. "My dear, sir, listen and take heed; women prefer a husband who, provided he is gentle and kind, commands. There is nothing they like less than a lover, or husband, who lets them make the decisions."

Justin frowned. "I have certainly observed that Libby allows Hal to make all the decisions with becoming meekness, but I had thought that a result of her adoration of him. I would prefer my wife to agree with my decisions after mature reflection."

"I'm sure she will," replied Mary, hiding a smile, "but trust me, in some things, she doesn't want a long-winded debate. Give her an ardent demand."

He digested this in stunned silence. "Am I to go back on my words of not three hours ago, then?" he asked doubtfully.

"Cleverly handled, I think so," she replied. "After all, you don't want to take a chance on losing her do you?"

"No, but it seems, so arbitrary," he said, seeming at loss as to how to proceed.

Mary smiled, "Just listen to me, and all will be well."

♣

A little later Bess, leaving her chamber in the state of indecision she'd been in ever since her talk with Justin, went along the corridor, as requested, to Mary's chamber. She was glad of the chance of talking to her elder sister, for she was never so undecided in her life. She had no idea of what to do for the best. On entering Mary's chamber, however, she found that she was not alone. Justin was there.

"Ah, Bess, see how I arrange everything for you." Mary came to meet her and gave her arm a little squeeze. "Now, I must away and see if these hunters are yet returned. You stay here with Justin and talk, but do make sure on leaving that you are not observed." She hurried off, leaving Bess looking bewildered.

"Here's luck," said Justin, coming to take her into his arms. "I didn't think to hold you again this quickly, love. Was Hal very sharp with you?"

"A little," she replied, returning his kiss, "but it has fallen out better than I dared hope. At least he accepts your presence."

"Yes," he hugged her again, and then lifted her chin to look into her face. "Bess, did you mean what you said to him, about never giving your consent to any proposal, but mine?"

She nodded slowly, "Yes, Justin."

"Does that mean you've reached a decision?" he asked tentatively.

"About a clandestine marriage? No," she said with a sigh. "I've thought and thought, Justin, until my head aches, but I cannot come to a decision. I want to be a good, dutiful daughter and sister, indeed, I do. Yet, I hate the thought of this marriage father has arranged. I know, if I refuse, he and Hal will be so angry with me, but I cannot consent to something so detrimental to all my hopes and wishes. It seems I must make a decision, but that decision is so difficult."

"Then I'll relieve you of the difficulty," he replied firmly, praying Mary's advice was sound. "Think no more on it, my love, for we are to be wed this evening."

"This evening?" she gasped in amazement.

"Yes, I'm sorry. I know I said I'd give you more time to consider, but quite frankly, love, I can't wait any longer. I want you, and I want you now, this very evening."

"Justin!" She looked shocked, but he noticed she blushed, too, and her eyes glowed.

"Disgraceful, isn't it?" he agreed, a wry smile playing about his mouth. "But, it seems if we are not to wed this evening, Mary's rector can't perform the ceremony until after Christmas and by that time—"

"—my father may have sent for me," she finished, seeing the sense in what he was proposing.

"I don't intend to let the chance of making you my wife slip so easily through my fingers," he said intently.

"So, love, I have the licence, and Mary has the rector. Do you have the courage to meet me in the chapel this evening, and let me make you mine forever?"

She blushed hotly, for there was no mistaking his meaning, or his determination. She looked up into his face, and her last doubt fled. "Oh, yes, Justin," she whispered breathlessly.

Chapter Six

In spite of Libby's fears, and she had many privately, Hal made no further mention of her brother as they withdrew to prepare for supper. The evening passed off better than could have been expected.

The presence of Justin, and the rector Thomas Featherstone, seemed to help weld the ill-assorted company into a whole. And, if Hal looked grim at the sight of Justin taking his old place beside Bess at the table, at least Justin's presence did much to shield her from the unpleasant advances of Geoffrey Soames.

Sir Edward appeared to pay as little attention to his latest guest as he had to any of the others, confining his conversation, as he had on the previous evening, almost exclusively to his cousins, Walter and Geoffrey Soames. They were soon deep in discussion of the chase and occasionally threw an odd remark to Ned, as if to underline that he was the only member of the Westwood family they could bear to speak to.

Sir Edward's general manner had little improved either, as was made plain when the meal was over. They'd withdrawn from the draughty hall, where the wind whipped keenly across the feet, into the snugger parlour, and Mary was attempting to make some amusement for her guests.

"Stop twittering, woman, and sit down," he snapped in an ungracious manner, as Mary timidly asked if any had a suggestion for the evening's entertainment. "The only entertainment we require is in a skin of wine. What we most certainly don't want, is you caterwauling on that damned lute of yours, if that's what you are about to suggest."

"Indeed, no sir," replied Mary with dignity. "I was more thinking that your Cousin Avis has a sweet singing voice and that Hal plays the lute better, by far, than I."

Cousin Avis subjected her pretty hostess to an avid scrutiny and shook her head. "I sing only in praise of the Lord, cousin," she replied in shocked tones. "I would scorn to use any gift given me in idle entertainment. The devil finds work for idle hands. You would all be better at your prayers! Besides," she added descending rapidly from these heights, "I could not sing even if I would, for I have the sore throat. Have you not observed I have it bound up in goose grease and flannel?"

Hal had been wondering at the odd smell, and had, indeed, ascribed it to Sir Edward, whose fingernails bore mute witness to the fact that he didn't weaken his excellent constitution by too close an association with water. Hal began to laugh at her oddness, and caught himself abruptly changing it to a cough adding apologetically, "I regret, Mary, that the injury to my shoulder means I cannot play either. What an unhealthy lot of guests you've assembled for the feast. I do trust we'll reach Twelfth Night with our numbers still intact. Surely, sister, your playing is equal to my own, and Bess sings well enough, especially if Libby is not too weary to sing with her."

"We'll have music enough tomorrow, when those damned wassailers from the village arrive, to make free with my food and drink," snarled Sir Edward. "Geoff, fetch that flagon of wine, and refill everyone's goblet. Well, Ned, my lad, what think you of my bitch? She seems to have taken quite a fancy to you."

Ned glanced to the spaniel, which sat at his feet, an expression of utter bliss on her face, as he unconsciously stroked her silken ears. "She's a good dog, sir," he replied politely. "Although to my mind a mite small for today's work. The staghounds were fleeter and had more staying power."

"Aye, I observed you took her up at one point," replied Sir Edward, "but she's dogged. She'll keep going, and is not usually so tardy, but that she's in whelp. I'll let you have the pick of the litter when they are born, for she drops a fine pup, which is more than can be said of the other bitches in this house!"

Hal saw Mary falter as she poured wine into a jug and her colour fade, whilst Guy Armstrong's fingers tightened about his goblet, until the knuckles showed white.

"You enjoyed good sport then, Sir Edward?" asked Hal with icy politeness.

"Aye," he replied carelessly. "A damned hard ride, over twenty miles if I am any judge, with your young brother leading the way. He showed us all a clean pair of heels, I can tell you, and doubtless would have brought down the stag, but that his horse went lame in taking a wall."

"Ah, so your quarry escaped you, Ned?" smiled Hal.

"Aye, for he was a canny fellow, with such a head on him as you never did see," said Ned. "At one point, I began to wonder if he were not Herne the Hunter himself, especially when my horse took a tumble over the wall like that. So I tied him to a tree, poor fellow, and gave chase on foot. I followed up the side of the hill, but by the time I reached the summit, near dead on my feet, the stag had given the dogs the slip and they were milling about seeking the scent. I could almost swear I saw him on the far side of the hill opposite but, you must understand, my sight was affected by the sweat in my eyes and shortness of breath."

"A full mile your brother ran, sir, keeping company with dogs," jibed Geoffrey Soames with a sneer. "I could scarce believe it."

"I don't doubt you could," Walter Soames agreed dryly, glancing sidelong at his own son, who presented a sorry sight compared to the vibrant, healthy Ned.

"You know my beast is not up to much, sir," complained Geoffrey, sensing contempt in his father's tone. "Last week it went lame. This week there was heat in one of its hocks. I've told you a hundred times I must have a new mount. God knows, I like the chase as well as the next man, but I cannot continue if I am to be mounted on inferior cattle. I fear I have not the taste for running after the quarry on foot, like young Mr Westwood."

While Geoffrey Soames fell into dispute with his father and uncle, as to whether it was the done thing to run the quarry to earth on foot "like a common groom", as he phrased it.

"So, the stag escaped the dogs," said Cecily whimsically. She sat on a stool at her sister's feet, carefully sorting and rewinding her tapestry wools, whilst Fanny listened to her betrothed's whispered conversation.

Ned glanced enigmatically to Cecily's vivacious little face. "Yes, why? Are you glad?"

"Well, sir, for your sake, no," she replied, as Hal, his temper ruffled by this blatant insult to his brother, joined in the men's dispute. "But for the stag's sake, yes. They are such magnificent creatures and I hate to think of them brought down by a pack of dogs, and then killed with knives. Hunting is such a barbaric sport."

Ned looked taken aback at this denunciation, "Well, yes, I suppose it is," he agreed, "although, men have always hunted."

"Yes, but that was for food. That's a different matter entirely," she replied at once.

"Cecily, you are impertinent to Mr Westwood," said her sister gently. "You have tantamount called him a barbarian!"

"Oh, I beg pardon, sir, I meant no offence," cried Cecily blushing.

Ned's glance narrowed as he looked across the room to where Geoffrey Soames sat, then he replied, "None taken where none is intended. Besides which, I don't know that I might agree with you. I've never looked at it like that before. I must confess, I do love the actual chase, only I truly enjoy it all the more when, as today, the beast is clever and makes an honourable escape."

She smiled up at him in approval, pleased at his words, and that he could be flexible enough to consider something in a different light.

Ned noticed her look and felt the flush creep into his freckled cheeks again. He had never before noticed how pretty a female's face could be. This girl wasn't a beauty like his step-mother, Jacqueline. Cecily reminded him strongly of Libby's kitten and, like that furry creature, not only had claws, but very much knew her own mind.

"So, sir, you are to have a new dog," Cecily continued in a chatty manner he found comfortable, as Justin skilfully guided the men's conversation into less troublesome waters. "Shall you like that?"

"Yes, yes, I will, we have several dogs at home, you understand, and Libby's cats, of course, but I shall enjoy having a spaniel."

"Do you live with your brother, Mr Westwood?" Fanny's fiance Rector Featherstone asked politely.

"Yes, I live with Libby and Hal most of the time,

with occasional visits to my other sisters, and my father in London. I do have a smaller property of my own, which abuts Hal's land, but we've put a tenant into that house until such time as I should—should" He hesitated over mentioning the word marriage, feeling suddenly, if he did, they would both guess the turmoil of his feelings. "—feel the need to live there," he added swiftly.

There was a short silence, then he continued, "I shall also inherit my father's fortune in due course. Hal, being the elder, had the good fortune to inherit Westwood, the home of our uncle. This being so, my father has promised to leave his money to me. Of course, I'll never be the owner of a handsome estate as Hal is, at least I sincerely hope not, for I am very fond of little Harry, but I shall not exactly be a pauper, especially when my father dies."

He shut his mouth with a snap, suddenly feeling foolish, wondering why he'd said so much. It was if he wished Fanny Armstrong to understand that he wasn't so bad a bargain for her sister. He flushed hotly again at the mere thought and turned back to his dog.

"Yes, Lady Jolyon has told us previously of your brother's good fortune," said Mistress Armstrong. "Your family seems to have fared better than ours in the last war, in that you managed to avoid the crippling fines which ruined us during the Protectorate. Poor Guy is next best thing to a pauper. We still struggle with our land, and how he'll ever find our dowries, I dread to think."

"Oh, we didn't manage to avoid the fines," sighed Ned. "My father insisted on fighting right to the very end. That's why his property is so much reduced. My uncle's ill health meant that he never fought after the Battle of Stow, so, of course, he fared rather better. He was also a far shrewder businessman than my father. But, in truth, it was Hal's marriage that finally restored our fortunes. Libby's father is a very wealthy man, and he was prepared to pay a huge dowry to see his daughter wed a gentleman."

"With far happier results than usually occurs from such a match it would seem," Mr Featherstone remarked, with a sigh.

Fanny Armstrong's eyes travelled thoughtfully to where Hal was leaning across Libby's chair, a look of concern on his handsome face. "Mistress Westwood ails, does she?"

"She lost a child back in the summer and is mid-way through another," said Ned, a trace of anxiety in his voice. "I don't know that she ails exactly, but Hal, rather naturally, is concerned."

Fanny Armstrong nodded her understanding, mentally assessing what she saw. Hal and Libby Westwood had but the one child from several pregnancies and the next in some doubt. To her mind, Master Ned sold himself short in this chancy world. It could well be that Ned would inherit a tidy fortune one day. She decided, for Cecily's sake, to cultivate the interest she glimpsed.

"As you are so fond of exercise, Mr Westwood, and with there being little likelihood, from what the gentlemen were saying, of more hunting because of the weather, I wonder if you'd not care to accompany my sister, and my brother Guy, of course, when they ride out to Thursby on St. Stephen's Day? It is a village a few miles to the south over the hill, an outpost, as Guy calls it, of our land. He says that as we are so close, it would be a pretty thing to call on his steward, such a worthy fellow, and his young family, to bring them the season's compliments. It may not have the excitement of the chase, but, if the rain should hold off, it can be a pleasant trip in good company."

Ned glanced shyly to Cecily, who had coloured prettily in embarrassment at this ruse, all thoughts of hunting banished. He could think of nothing likely to appeal to him more.

"Why, thank you, ma'am, I should indeed like to do so," he said politely. "And provided neither my brother nor sister require me, I'll be glad to go."

A small silence fell in the solar at this point and Justin hastily filled it before either their host, or his kin, could be offensive. "The castle is very old, I believe, Lady Jolyon. Tell me, do you have a ghost here?"

"Why, yes, we do," replied Mary at once. "One of my predecessors at the time of the Crusades, or so the tale goes, is known as the Lady of Sidworth Castle."

"Have you seen her walk, ma'am?" Cecily asked, her eyes widening in horror.

"No," confessed Mary smiling. "I have never seen her, but 'tis said others have."

"Are you one of their number, Sir Edward?" Justin asked, hoping to include him in the conversation, for he noticed the party always seemed to be split.

"No, I have not," he replied ungraciously. "The whole tale is nothing but lies. Lady of Sidworth Castle, indeed! The Trollop of Sidworth is more my guess."

"Will you not recount the tale anyway, Mary?" asked Libby. She cast her host an unfavourable look, thinking how deplorably his manner compared with Hal's.

"Well, if you are all interested," she said, a little doubtfully. "It would seem the Lord of Sidworth Castle at that time took to himself a beautiful new bride, whom he loved right well. On the day of his wedding, a crone arrived to tell him that he'd lose that which he loved best, if he didn't keep the vow that his father had sworn in return for his birth. This vow was that his son should go on a crusade to the Holy Land before the year was out. Well, he lingered all spring and summer with his bride, putting off his decision to go, but as the autumn came, his conscience wouldn't let him rest, for he began to fear that he, too, might lack an heir if he didn't fulfil the bargain. As he dwelt upon these matters, his affection for his bride grew almost to an obsession, so that he became jealous of his lovely wife, and began to suspect her virtue. By the time the first frost came, he'd decided to go on a crusade. But he also decided to lock his wife in the top-most chamber of the highest tower of Sidworth Castle, and he left implicit instructions that she was not to be allowed out, nor to be seen by any, until his return, the following spring."

"Oh, how very wicked!" cried Libby. "Why, 'tis plain he didn't love her at all."

"Indeed," agreed Mary, "and foolish too, for the Lord had not been gone above a fortnight, when the plague came to the castle, striking down all within her walls. Those who were not killed outright, were too ill to recollect their lady, until it was too late."

"Oh, did she starve to death?" cried Cecil in horror.

"No, worse still. She went mad, so they say, what with the hunger, and the fear of loneliness. She threw herself from the topmost window, crashing to her death at the very feet of her returning lord. It seems as he was about to embark for the Holy Land, he suffered a change of heart, knowing he couldn't bear to be parted from his love for so long, and so he had returned post haste, in time to witness her tragic end."

"Oh, how sad!" Bess sighed.

"A fitting end to a foolish slut," growled Sir Edward. "Depend upon it, there was no smoke without fire."

"A just end, for a possessive nature," said Hal sharply, "but a sorry one for the sweet lady. Did her lord go off into a melancholy and never speak again?"

"No," Mary laughed bitterly. "He married the daughter of a neighbour within a month, and thereafter produced fifteen children. The lords of Sidworth Castle are known to have no heart." Her bright-eyed smile swept about to include everyone. "The only consolation for the poor lady's ghost was that none of the sons survived infancy, and the castle passed to the lord's distant cousin on his death."

"Poor, poor lady," Bess shuddered.

"Yet, more still, poor second wife," said Libby, hugging little Harry to her. "How very dreadful, to lose her sons through no real fault of her own."

"Yes," mused Hal, "you know, if I'd been the second wife, I'd have had some conditions attached to the wedding vows."

"Which conditions, Hal?" Mary asked smiling.

"Well, first off, I'd insist on a vow never to go off on a crusade," he said, with a half laugh.

"Aye," said Ned, adding with a grin, "and I'd be sure to have a second set of all the keys to the castle."

"I think I'd just insist he didn't love me too well," Bess said quietly.

"One must consider, she cannot have been over-scrupulous herself," remarked Justin. "Or she would not have agreed to marry him so very quickly."

"Unless her father insisted," murmured Bess, her eyes dark. "Recollect, a female cannot always marry as she will."

Fanny Armstrong, glancing to Cecily's face, decided she'd probably heard enough. Fanny was tempted to allow her to bask in the sunshine of Ned Westwood's admiration, but she concluded, as Justin enquired as to the exact spot in which the lady was supposed to walk, if Cecily heard anymore, neither of them would get a wink of sleep. Fanny had no hesitation in reminding her sister that the hour was advanced, and summarily packed her off to bed.

The departure of the Armstrong sisters broke up the party. Libby, who had long been weary, took the opportunity to follow them. Cousin Avis and Bess were not far behind. Staying only to see her guests needed nothing further, Mary was the last of the ladies to leave.

Guy Armstrong, Hal noted with concern and disapproval, did not waste much time in quitting the company either. The men were more determined to remain. Ned and Justin discussing with the rector the day's hunt, whilst Sir Edward and his kinsmen seemed settled down for a night of drinking. Hal, who wanted to speak to Sir Edward, viewed this development with dismay, but had forgotten the effects of fresh air upon the huntsmen.

The yawns began with Justin, who had his own reasons for wanting everyone abed. In no time Sir Edward and his cousin were struggling against yawns, whilst Geoffrey, stupefied with wine, lay slumped back in a chair, snoring loudly.

Ned, who wasn't feeling particularly tired, but rather wanted to go to bed to think about Cecily, finally made a move. This prompted Walter Soames, who got unsteadily to his feet and kicked his son, waking him with a start.

"Sir Edward," said Hal, as Geoffrey began to curse loudly. "May I have a few words with you before we retire?" He would have preferred to speak to his sister's husband when he was completely sober, but hadn't yet had the opportunity of finding him so.

"You may have as many words as you choose," he replied unpleasantly, "but whether they'll be to your liking is another matter."

Hal nodded, unwilling to waste another civil word on him, and waited patiently whilst Geoffrey Soames took his drunken exit. He couldn't deny that Mary's lines had not fallen pleasantly. It was plain Sir Edward was coarse, ill mannered and appeared to be as brutal as she claimed. His heart had gone out to his sister many times in the course of the evening, and he was determined to do his best to improve her lot.

"Well, what do you want?" demanded Sir Edward, as Geoffrey was heard to stumble on the stairs and curse audibly. "'Tis time we were all abed."

"Indeed," said Hal coldly, "I'll be as brief as possible. You have spoken several times this evening, sir, in so marked a manner as to give me, along with several other discourtesies, the distinct impression that you do not hold my sister Mary, your wife, in very high esteem."

Sir Edward laughed bitterly and finished off the remainder of his wine. "You are correct, young man. I don't."

"I see. Can you tell me the reasons thereof?" asked Hal. He was determined the other's rudeness would not cause him to lose his temper.

"Reasons?" Sir Edward grunted and got to his feet. "Aye, I can tell you reasons. I was sold a bad bargain, Mr Westwood, a bad bargain."

"In what respect?" asked Hal.

"Your father promised me a good, meek, pliable, fertile wife," he returned. "A wife who would give me a son every year for the next ten years. Instead, I am left with a whining, useless piece, who holds herself too high to grace my bed!"

"She has refused to accept your advances?" asked Hal quickly.

"Nay, she's too sly for that," he snarled. "There's more than one way of sending a man from your bed, if you've no mind for him. She'd never dare deny me, for she knows I'd beat her again, as is my right, but I don't trouble with her now. Her, with her sighs and martyred airs; I like a wench with a bit of welcome about her, not a graven image, who lies abed long-suffering, wrinkling her disdainful nose at my approach!"

Hal, whose nostrils had twitched at his sour, wine-sodden breath, which had encompassed them, felt all the more for his poor sister. "Whilst none would deny your right to chastise an erring wife, within reason, Sir Edward, I must tell you to your face that, as I understand the matter, your treatment of my sister has been brutally excessive. In short, I gather that you have frequently beaten her, restrained her in her chamber for lengthy periods, even on occasions refusing her sustenance. This being the case, I am compelled to tell you that, should such instances as these ever occur again, I shall have no hesitation in taking you to law."

"Take a man to law for beating his wife?" he sneered. "You'd be laughed out of court."

"Nevertheless, I would do so, and I do not think it would suit you, Sir Edward, to be called to account for your actions. Furthermore, should I have any report of such occurrences again, I shall remove my sister Mary from your home, and enter a suit for divorce, citing gross cruelty on your part."

Sir Edward glared at him, hating him all the more for his erudite speech, his unassailable calm, his noble looks and his iron determination.

"You can suit yourself," he muttered. "I care neither way. Her, she's not worth the fighting for. A useless, barren, bitch she is. No good to man, nor beast."

Hal lost some of his calm. "Tell me, Sir Edward, how

many sons, or daughters come to that, did your first wife give you?"

"None," he snarled. "A puling, sickly creature she was. Forever ailing or miscarrying! I was glad to see the end of her, when the childbed fever took her."

"And mistresses?" asked Hal sharply, hardly endeared to the man by these words. "A strong hardy fellow like yourself, must have had a dozen or more woman over the years. They had sons, had they?"

"Some may, some not; What are you inferring?" he demanded, unable in his drunken state, to keep pace with Hal's quicker wits.

"None you can lay claim to then," murmured Hal. "That doesn't strike you as strange, Sir Edward, in all these years? You make haste to call my sister barren, yet I begin to wonder if it is she who is at fault."

"My first wife had a dozen miscarriages, aye, and still-births, too. All this, it is none of my fault. The seed is set, but will not ripen," he cried wrathfully.

"Unless, of course, the seed be awry, and the fruit cannot safely ripen," Hal retorted.

"You're a fine one to talk," shouted Sir Edward. "What have you to show for your years of marriage? One puny boy, whose life doesn't look worth the pur-chase, and sickly lass! Aye, and your uncle fared no better. 'Tis not the Jolyons who are barren, 'tis Westwood ruined stock!"

"You are wondering from the point," said Hal firmly. He was determined not to deteriorate into a trading of insults. "I came tonight to inform you I will not countenance the ill-treatment of my sister any longer. Any repeat of it, and I shall seek a legal injunction to restrain you. I have no more to say on the matter, and so will bid you goodnight."

With a bow, Hal strode swiftly from the chamber. He left the older man to furiously call for his servant, all the while ranting about jumped up, impudent, young jackanapes. Hal paid this no heed, but hastened up the stairs to the tower room not convinced, in his mind, he'd achieved anything.

Chapter Seven

As Hal lay in bed, the conviction he'd done more harm than good grew on him, and when he did finally fall asleep, it was to dream of Mary in distress. He awoke later with a start, which disturbed Libby, and froze in position, while she drifted back to sleep. His mind began to race over his problems again, until his head throbbed and his shoulder burned and ached. Finally, feeling he could be still no longer, he slid from the bed fearful of rousing Libby. Slipping on his boots and thick cloak against the biting cold, he went in search of a drink.

He recollected how Mary had said a jug of ale was usually left out at the court cupboard in the Great Hall overnight, for those who could not face the rigours of the dark without some refreshment.

Hal lit his candle from the lantern burning on the stairs, and trod down to the floor below, wondering what o'clock it was. Although he felt certain he'd been asleep for hours, somehow in the complete darkness, he did not think it near dawn. His way led him past the door to his sister Bess's chamber, and he was mildly surprised to see a light under it as he approached. This was nothing, however, to the amazement he felt as he drew level, and a burst of laughter came from within.

It did not take him a split second to identify the voices as that of a man, and also his sister Mary. Instinctively he thought of Guy Armstrong, and he debated what he should do. By rights, he knew he should walk in on them, Bess was, after all, nominally in his care, but he shrank from the embarrassment of such a step. Then, as he stood in a quandary, there was another burst of laughter, which decided him. God knew, he shied from this sort of involvement, but he owed it to his family, to make the couple see sense, before it all ended in scandal and disaster.

Even so, he did beat a tattoo on the oaken panels as he entered, swiftly closing the door behind him. Then he stopped short and was forced to lean against it, as if for support, as his astounded gaze took in the sight of his sister Bess. She was sitting, banked up against the pillows of the curtained bed alongside Justin, a cup of wine in her hand. Mary was in the act of handing another cup to Justin, and Guy Armstrong stood with his cup raised, clearly he was just about to pledge a toast.

"Hal!" cried Mary. She whipped round so quickly as to slop the red wine on the white sheets.

"Damnation!" exclaimed Justin, turning red in the face, whilst Bess, with one glance at the incredulity and anger dawning on her brother's shocked face, gave an inarticulate cry of dismay, and buried her head in Justin's shoulder.

"Now the fat is truly in the fire!" remarked Guy Armstrong comically, and he drank off his cup of wine.

"Are you mad?" demanded Hal blankly, as his eyes went from the couple in the bed, to Mary. "Are you dead to all sense of common decency? By heaven! Can I believe my eyes? Are you so far gone along the road to destruction and degradation that you must connive at your sister's downfall? Have you truly helped Bess into a trollop's bed, to soothe your own feelings of guilt?"

"Now, just a moment," said Guy, all the good nature falling from his face. "How dare you speak to Mary like that?"

"I dare because she is the slut you've made her," snapped Hal. "Don't take that tone with me, my fine fellow, for you are every bit as guilty as she!"

"I think perhaps you should know, Hal," said Justin, looking up from where he'd been trying to console Bess, as Guy turned crimson, and spluttered over a reply. "That your sister and I were married earlier this evening, and that I, like Guy, take a dim view of the intemperate manner in which you are addressing both your sisters."

"Married!" cried Hal, his jaw dropping. "Married? How? Where?"

"Here in the chapel, by the parish priest, who will shortly become my brother-in-law," replied Guy, tartly and with evident satisfaction.

"It cannot be legal!" cried Hal.

"On the contrary," said Justin dryly. "I have taken great pains to ensure it is."

"Yet neither of you have my, or my father's, consent," Hal said blankly.

"No," agreed Justin reluctantly, "but under common law, the marriage, duly solemnised and witnessed by two persons, still stands."

Hal continued to stare at them stunned, as if rooted to the ground.

"Not only solemnised, but also consummated, Hal," Mary spoke with some spite, for his harsh words had touched her on the raw. "It is what is called a 'fate accompli'. You'd better accept it."

"I—I cannot believe it," he stammered, adding in growing anger, "No more will I accept it. No more will our father." The mention of his father seemed to crystallise his thoughts, for he turned on Justin with some venom. "Yes, I begin to see it now! You think you've tricked us finely, don't you, with this talk of common law, but I'll see you worsted yet! You are not the only lawyer in the land. We'll see this is settled yet—at the Court of Arches—the highest court, if need be."

Justin turned pale and his mouth went dry in shock, "Certainly, if you feel the need to drag your family name through the mud."

"It won't be my name, but yours, which goes through the mud," cried Hal furiously. "I'll not rest until I see you ruined."

"That will most certainly endear you to Libby!" Mary remarked sarcastically.

Hal bit back a reply, his anger fanned to even greater heights by the truth of this. He drew himself up imperiously, cast them all a look of scorching contempt, and stalked from the chamber, slamming the door after him.

"My, but he's a magnificent creature, isn't he?" Guy chuckled, his eyes wide with amazement, "With those looks, and that temper, he quite terrifies me! I must confess, I'm glad he is your brother, Mary, and not mine."

"I am not glad he is my brother," snapped Mary. "I vow I've never known such an insufferable, conceited, arrogant, self-righteous bore in all my life!"

Justin gave a reluctant laugh, for his thoughts had been running along the same lines, but as Bess finally raised her face from her husband's shoulder, to reveal streaming eyes, he said fairly, "No, he's not that bad. At least, not usually. He can be irritatingly pompous, I agree, until he loses his temper, then you have to look out, but he's a sound fellow at heart. One I'd trust my life to, once he's over the tantrums and prickles."

"No, no, you are all wrong," Bess cried tearfully. "He's an absolute darling, who'd do anything for us all. I've hurt and disappointed him. I know he'll never forgive me."

"Well, it was either that, or hurting and disappointing Justin," Mary said practically, unimpressed by this romantic view. "Not to mention being miserable for the rest of your life, wed to that beast Jack Petherbridge. So you'd best make up your mind to endure Hal's sulks."

"You'd also better consummate this marriage, or it isn't legal," said Guy Armstrong with a grin. "Come, my love, our presence is no longer required. We'll take our wine, and leave our bride and groom in peace."

Mary bent over her sister, smoothing back her long, fine hair and hugged her. "Put Hal from your mind," she whispered. "We'll tackle him together tomorrow after the feast, when he is relaxed with wine, and we'll have Libby on our side, too. No more tears now, remember, 'tis unlucky for a bride to weep. You don't want Justin to think you regret it already, do you?"

With a kindly kiss for her sister, and an approving nod for her new brother-in-law, she followed Guy to the door. Mary paused to extract a posy of herbs and a few fragile flowers from her waistband, which she threw onto the bed. "Oh, I nearly forgot, a nosegay to bring you fine sons! Here's rosemary for remembrance, and rue for grace, and others for fertility. Well, goodnight! God bless!"

Justin stole a sidelong glance at his bride as the door closed behind them. "I'm sorry, Bess," he said softly. "I'd hoped we'd have managed better than this, but Hal seems to be everywhere today."

She hastily mopped up a stray tear with her sleeve cuff. "But no longer here and now, Justin," she replied, with a watery smile.

"True," he agreed, his ready-grin hovering. "After all, what's the use in crying over spilt milk?" He slid his arm about her slender shoulders and drew her closer to him. "We are married," he said gently. "None can change that now, and that is the main thing."

"Yes, it is," she replied "so put out the candle, my love."

Hal, meanwhile, had found his cup of ale and drunk it down in one. Another cup followed, yet, he was still so furiously angry, that on his return to his chamber, he forgot to either effect a silent entry, or dim his candle.

Libby was awoken and sat up at once. "Is that you, Hal?" she cried, blinking in the light of the candle.

"Damn," he muttered, annoyed at waking her. "Yes, and I'm sorry, Libby."

"What is it, Hal?"she asked quickly, having taken one look at his thunderous face.

He sat down heavily on the bed. "Nothing that signifies," he muttered unconvincingly.

She leaned across to clasp his shoulder. "What is it?" she repeated, bewildered.

More annoyed with himself than ever, for he'd not meant to say anything about it to her, yet finding he must tell someone, or burst, he said, in a voice he kept rigidly calm, "I've just come from a bed-chamber I assumed to be my sister Bess's, where I found her abed with your brother. They were drinking a toast with Mary and her paramour, Armstrong. I was informed Bess was married earlier this evening to Justin!"

"Married! Bess—and—and—"

"Justin, yes!" he snarled over his shoulder.

She sat back in the bed, in amazement, staring at his averted back. "Oh dear," she said inadequately.

"I still cannot believe it," he cried, his anger growing, yet again, as he reviewed the scene. "I still feel as if the power of coherent thought has been taken from me! How could he do this? How could she?"

"They—they are desperate, Hal," she murmured. "Don't you see that? It is the action of desperate lovers."

"But to dare to come here, to my sister's home? To make the pretence of attending the festivities that he might be with you? To take my hand in peace as he did? Even then he was planning to trick me like this! Oh, a pretty fool I shall look before my father!"

"Bess is not in your care, Hal, but Mary's," she suggested tentatively.

"Aye, and I should have removed her from this place, as soon as I saw what manner of woman she was," he retorted furiously. "Mary's care indeed! She has plotted and connived all this with them both. She's been hand in glove with your brother throughout. Although why, I cannot see, unless it be a wicked desire to see her sister's reputation is as ruined as is her own."

"No, Hal," she grasped his shoulder again, making him face her. "No, Mary has done this thing because she loves Bess, because she doesn't want her to endure the misery she has. She told you all this yesterday when we arrived, only you didn't listen. Surely you must be able to understand the despair of Bess, loving Justin as she does, about to be tied to another man? I am certain you must, for did you not experience similar feelings when we were wed? Can you not feel with Justin's anger, to see the woman he adores tied for life to another man? Surely you witnessed such feelings knowing Jacqueline was married to your father, didn't you? Surely then you can comprehend something of their anguish."

"I—I never adored—or loved Jacqueline," he stammered, colouring. "I'll not deny I was a young fool, and infatuated by her beauty, but I never loved her. The feelings I had for Jacqueline were pure lust."

"Perhaps they were," she agreed, "but you were not sure of your feelings at our wedding were you? Did you not then experience the same sense of despair which has overtaken Justin and Bess?"

"I do not recollect, and if I did, they soon faded in the face of your steady affection, Libby. It was you who showed me what true love really is. This blind passion which Bess and Justin feel is nothing but a hollow sham."

She shook her head. "When one is in love, Hal, one doesn't speak of steady affection," she observed sadly. "I have never loved you with steady affection, but with plain, unadulterated adoration from the moment you took my hand, and spoke to me in my cousin's garden."

He reddened again, knowing in his heart this was true. "What is this you say? That there is only one way to love?" he asked sharply. "That although I've stumbled on a path, making wrong moves and many mistakes, that I don't truly love you now?"

She looked up into his handsome face, full of shadows in the candlelight, her own softening instinctively. "No, I think we have been incredibly fortunate. As you say, we've stumbled our way to happiness with each other, but it so easily could have gone awry, Hal. And don't you think, having found so precious a gift, that we should help others on their way? Come, my love, tell me true. Do you believe Bess has but a wild infatuation for Justin, that his love will not endure?"

"It is beside the point, what I believe now," he replied irritated by this appeal to his emotions. "They have deliberately disobeyed my father's instructions, and claim to be married. It shall be for the law to decide."

"The law?" Libby asked, in blank dismay.

"Aye, your brother quoted common law at me. He assured me he'd taken great care to make the marriage legal, but his is not the only opinion in the land. I shall see. I shall seek legal counsel of my own, damn it!" He added as a thought occurred to him. "I should have not left them together. I should have insisted on Bess leaving with me. I wonder if I have inadvertently weakened our case?" He made as if to move, and she caught his hand, arresting him.

"Hal, you cannot mean this," she cried in horror. "You cannot seriously be thinking of taking Justin to law?"

"I have no choice," he replied firmly. "I cannot allow this flouting of my father's authority to go unchallenged. He would demand I do something."

"Your father is not here," she returned, exasperated, "and he will never take the trouble to go to law, if you do not back him. Oh, I grant you, he'll rant and shout at the housetops for a while. Then he'll sit down to hammering out an advantageous settlement with my father. I have no doubt, Hal. This is Bess and Justin we are speaking of, people I thought we both loved. You cannot do this to them!"

"I not only can, I must, it is my duty," he replied, shaking off her restraining hand.

"No, Hal," she cried and caught hold of his cloak firmly. "No, I say, you must not, you cannot, think of separating them! They love each other, and they are legally married."

"So your brother claims," he snapped. "And fool that I was, so bewildered and taken aback, that I did not so much as challenge it. My God, how could I have been so stupid? I am a purblind fool. Don't you see? It could all be lies! I'll wager ten to one they aren't married at all, that he has merely taken her, knowing that once she lost her virginity to him, we'd be clamouring for them to be wed. I must go back and fetch Bess. She can sleep remainder of the night here with you, and tomorrow, at first light, we'll all leave this house of iniquity."

"No, Hal," she grabbed on his cloak, arresting his departure. "No," she cried desperately, "I beg you won't even think of being so inhuman. Would Bess, your sweet sister Bess, consent to bed with Justin without marriage? Do you think your gentle sister so lost? Never! Would Justin, my dear brother, who is as honourable as you, sink to something so despicable and underhand? No! You must be wrong. I am certain if Justin says so, they are legally married. And, if that is the case, not only would it be wicked and despicable, but you'd have no right to part them."

He looked down at her, his eyes cold. "You seem so very sure of the case, Libby. I ask myself if you did not know of the event beforehand, too."

She fell back from him, releasing her grip on his cloak, her face stricken. "No, I did not," she replied, her tone echoing her amazement he could even suggest such a thing.

"Well, whether you did or you didn't, you've made your position pretty clear," he returned roughly, the sense of guilt he felt warring with what he knew to be his duty. "Plainly you side with them in this matter. In effect, you would have me betray my father's trust in me, and do nothing."

"I would have you allow the understanding and love I know to be in your heart win through," she replied, tears gathering in her eyes. "If you truly love me, Hal, as you say you do, you'd not subject me to this pain."

"That is not fair," he cried, stung. "This is not a personal matter, Libby, but one of principle. We cannot allow my father's authority to be flouted in this manner."

"There you are wrong, Hal. There are no principles in this matter. We are talking of simple love, not high-flown words and fine-sounding phrases, but love," she said, tears now streaming down her face. "If you love me as you claim, if you love Bess as you say, if you have the slightest respect, or affection, for Justin, you'll let them be!"

"I cannot do that, Libby," he cried in dismay. "You must

see that I cannot stand by and allow this to happen."

"Then I have my answer," she replied, looking away from him.

"You are being unreasonable," he cried, beginning to get angry with her now. "I'll not allow you to hold me to ransom like this."

"I do not have to be reasonable," she snapped. "I am a woman. I see no merit, whatsoever, in logic that would part two people I love dearly, and who worship each other. No more can I respect a man, who parts them in the name of reason."

His face hardened. "Then 'tis plain you and I must agree to differ, but do not think I shall bow my head to your threats, Libby, for I know I am right."

"And I feel in my heart you are wrong,"she whispered.

He stared at her, feeling his world turn upside down and a gulf opened between them. It seemed he must stand alone against his family, without even the security of knowing his wife believed in him. "You are, of course, entitled to your opinion," he replied at his stateliest. "However, as your husband— and master—I must demand it is kept to yourself. In public, I insist we present a united front, and that front is that we neither approve, nor acknowledge, this supposed marriage."

She met his eyes mutinously, knowing he had the right to demand it of her. "If I must accede to this outrageous demand," she replied, "you must comply with mine—that nothing further is done in this matter until morning. I absolutely insist that they are, at the very least, to have one night together."

"I shall concede nothing," he returned curtly, his eyes flashing. "You have no right to make demands of me, and if you do not do as I bid you, I shall keep you locked here in this chamber until our departure. Do you understand me?"

She stared at him, taken aback and a little frightened, for never before had he spoken to her in such a manner. No more had she any doubt, in his present black temper, he'd be as good as his word.

"I understand you,"she whispered, her lips trembling at her own boldness, "but I dare you to go against my wishes."

He glared at her furiously for a few seconds, his breath taken away by her audacity. Then, he turned on his heel, snatching up his candle, and went from the chamber.

Chapter Eight

Ned awoke early on Christmas morn, as he always did. He got from his bed swiftly, his thoughts, like his dreams, full of Cecily. He dressed grinning at the sight of her brother spread-eagled on the bed, still snoring loudly.

Never had he felt so happy. Not only was it Christmas, but he was filled with joy. All his life he'd been conscious of being alone, different from other boys. It wasn't until Hal returned from exile, that he understood what an isolated childhood he'd had.

Whilst he'd been happier these last years as the two of them worked together, often, when Libby had been present, he'd felt more alone than ever. Now, he knew instinctively his world was complete. Cecily squared the circle.

He knew it was yet early and, as he eased the shutter back quietly, the strange white light told him his cup of happiness overflowed. Leaving Guy Armstrong to sleep off his late night, he went in search of company, taking care, as he went down the creaking stairs, not to rouse those still abed.

He stopped dead at the foot of the tower to stare in amazement at the sight of his brother. Hal was sleeping in a most uncomfortable attitude on a settle at the head of the stairs to the hall below. "Hal?" he said shaking his arm, "Hal, is aught amiss with Libby?"

Hal opened his eyes and flinched at the sudden pain in his stiff neck.

"What? What is that you say?" he demanded thickly. "Oh, God, what time is it?"

"Near eight o'clock on the snowiest Christmas I can remember," replied Ned, frowning at him puzzled. "What do you here? Is Libby ill?"

"Libby? No merely in a—" he said as he sat up with a groan. "Did you say snow?"

"Yes, did you not hear the wind?" Ned asked. He was still puzzled, but suddenly realised there must have been a quarrel.

"No, I had a tempest of my own," muttered Hal as he dropped his head to his hands. "Be a good lad, Ned, and run and fetch me a mug of ale from the buffet in the hall, will you? My head is aching damnably."

Hal pulled his cloak about him more securely, and

bent to massage his cold feet, as Ned ran swiftly down the stairs. He was staring gloomily into nothing, when the boy returned with the drink. "Nobody is about yet, but a few servants," Ned remarked brightly. "I've looked at the snow, it must be at least a foot deep."

"A foot!" cried Hal in horror. "My God, has it settled then?"

"Settled and frozen," said Ned, laughing. "We should see some sport today. Guy Armstrong was telling me the moat often freezes, and that it makes capital skating."

Hal shook his head, as if to free it from sleep and pain. "There'll be no sport for us today, Ned. We must leave at once."

"Leave?" asked Ned. He was conscious of a sinking feeling in his stomach, as he realised that he'd not see Cecily again. "But why?"

"Why?" repeated Hal, "Because, my brother, last night with the aid of Mary, and your friend Armstrong, our sister Bess was married to Justin Danvers."

"Justin?" cried Ned. "But—but Father forbade the match."

"Aye, and I've been finely tricked," Hal replied resentfully. "Just how much, I am not sure, but I caught them abed together."

"Father will not be pleased," remarked Ned, opening his eyes wide at this, and adding after a moment's thought, "Why must we leave?"

"We must take Bess away. The marriage cannot be legal, and I'll not remain in a house where we are so insulted."

Ned frowned. "As I see it, the insult is to Sir Edward," he remarked. "It's his hospitality which has been violated. In truth, if Justin has wedded and bedded Bess, I don't see what we can do about it. She can't make another marriage, and after all, father did initially give his consent. It would be better to accept it, and not make a fuss. Only think of what the gossips will make of it, if you try to contest the marriage."

Hal could have groaned in dismay. His last thought, as he drifted off into a fitful sleep, when his fury had finally died down, was that Ned was sure to side with him, that Ned was impartial. "I cannot help the scandal," he stated firmly. "Bess has brought this upon herself. I shall insist that she leaves with us."

"Then you'll be making a fool of yourself," said Ned bluntly. "How far do you think we'd get in this weather with a reluctant bride, a pregnant woman and a small child? We'd be lucky to make it to the nearest inn, without dying of cold."

Hal glared at his outspoken brother. "I cannot help the difficulties, we must make an attempt to leave."

"Don't be a fool, Hal," he replied crisply. "We can't possibly leave. The risk to Libby, to her child and to little Harry, is too great. And for what end? So you can salve your offended sensibilities? Do talk sense. We've no choice, but to remain here. Sir Edward's old groom was bringing in the wood for the fires, and he says the sky is full of snow, and that the crow is low in tree or something, which means more storms. Face it, we're stuck here for the next few days and, quite frankly, that being the case, I'd prefer any scandal to be kept from Sir Edward and his family."

"Are you saying we must condone this marriage?" asked Hal angrily.

"I'm saying if we must all remain here, and I do believe we must, then I'd sooner rub along with everyone in at least a semblance of harmony," replied Ned bluntly.

"I cannot tolerate this situation," said Hal, "I have been tricked. Brought here to lend countenance to a disgraceful sham of a marriage, which I cannot approve."

"I don't see why," said Ned, "You did approve of it, until father went back upon his word. I like Justin. He's a good enough fellow, even if he is prosy, and we owe him much, after saving father from the gallows, as he did."

"He didn't save father from the gallows. I got a pardon from the king. There was never any chance of father going to the gallows. And a good fellow? To persuade your sister to enter into a clandestine marriage? If it was a marriage," snapped Hal.

"Well, Bess is no fool," replied Ned. "I can't see her entering into a marriage that isn't legal."

"I cannot believe you take this so calmly," cried Hal. "This is your sister we speak of. We would be quite within our rights to challenge Justin to a duel, or to horsewhip him."

"A duel? With me as your second, and Libby as his, whilst Bess weeps in the foreground?" suggested Ned ironically. "Come down off your high horse, Hal, this is family we are talking of. You can take no action against Justin. He is Libby's brother."

"Aye, and so he knew," snarled Hal, "when he began this. I have been taken advantage of."

"And I thought Bess the injured maid," Ned remarked slyly. As Hal glared at him, he added, "Come, Hal, see reason. What can we do, but hold our tongues?"

Hal returned no reply to this unanswerable question, burying his face in his mug of ale, and muttering under his breath.

"What we'd better do," said Ned, after a few moments silence. "Is to—" He stopped abruptly as a door opened onto the landing, and Justin stepped out.

At the sight of the two brothers, he looked uncomfortable, but resolutely advanced upon them, saying as easily as possible, "Merry Christmas, Hal, Ned."

"Merry Christmas, brother," said Ned with emphasis.

Justin's colour deepened. "I see you are—are—aware of the circumstances," he began uncertainly. "And I'd like to take this opportunity to—to—"

"Excuse me," Hal got to his feet handing Ned his mug. "I must make myself ready for the day." And he walked away without another word.

"I guess he and Libby have quarrelled," said Ned, looking after him. "He bears the mark of a man who has slept the night on a hard settle."

"Oh, don't say so," said Justin in dismay. "I cannot bear that Libby and he should be at odds over this."

"Well, they are bound to be," said Ned prosaically. "I was just about to say to Hal that we three had better meet and talk, later this morning."

"I rather gather that will be an impossibility, as Hal seems to be intent on cutting me," said Justin, with a sigh.

"Well, you have made him look pretty silly," said Ned bluntly, "and you know how prickly his pride is."

"I could be said to have made you look silly, too," suggested Justin.

"I'm not bothered how I look. I'm not the heroic type," grinned Ned, "but I am concerned about the scandal. I don't like Sir Edward, or his family. I'd rather they knew nothing of this."

"What a practical youngster you are, Ned!" exclaimed Justin, much relieved by his attitude.

"It's as well one of us has his feet on the ground," he agreed. "We'll meet at ten in my chamber. Guy Armstrong should be about by then, although, God knows, it was late enough, in all conscience, when he finally came to bed. The chamber is at the top of the tower there, and we should, at least, be undisturbed and not overheard."

Chapter Nine

Mary looked up quickly and managed a wan smile, as Libby entered the Great Hall, which was filled with reflected light from the snow, and looked drabber than ever. "Merry Christmas, Libby, Merry Christmas, Harry," she said to the little boy Libby was leading by the hand. "Come, sit here close to the fire, for the wind is finding all the gaps today."

"Merry Christmas, Aunt Mary," Harry lisped, in reply to Libby's prompting. He also directed an angelic smile at the only other occupant of the breakfast table, Mistress Soames.

"Oh, isn't he a darling," sighed Mary. She helped him scramble to the bench beside her, whilst Libby paused at the buffet, to fill a bowl with bread and warmed milk. "Did you sleep well, Libby?" asked Mary, casting her swollen eyes and unsmiling face a worried glance.

"No, did you not?" asked Libby as she set the bowl before her little son and sat down to spoon-feed him.

"I must own, the wind kept me awake," replied Mary, looking distressed, as she glanced to Avis Soames in dismay. "I am sorry so few of us have chosen to grace my table this morn," she continued hurriedly, "I rather fear my husband still sleeps off the excess of exercise he took yesterday, and probably the excess of wine consumed last night. Whereas your husband has the headache, does he not, Avis? And Geoffrey is just a slug-a-bed. The men of your family, however, Libby, have all broken their fast and gone about their business." She forced a bright smile. "No need to worry," she added, as neither woman spoke. "No doubt we'll all come together for church presently."

"I shall not attend service this morning," said Libby quietly. "My disturbed night has had an unfortunate effect on my stomach, making me sickly and, in any case, I would not care to walk so far in this snow." She glanced up and read condemnation in Mistress Soames's eyes. "My physician insists I must not over tire myself, if I am to carry this child to full term."

"The devil sets traps for us all, Mistress Westwood," said Mistress Soames. "You'd do better to fear for your immortal soul, than you earthly body. It seems it is fashionable these days to be a fine lady and lie a bed with bellyache, rather than do one's duty." She turned her eyes on Mary's pallid face, noting how she crumbled the bread between anxious fingers. "If I were mistress of this castle, I'd look to my cook. For, if that fish we ate last night were fresh, I know nothing of the matter. One can never be sure of fish this far inland, at this time of the year."

"Libby is sickly because of her child and a disturbed night," replied Mary crossly. "There was naught amiss with the fish, and I doubt any of my guests would have relished salt herring at Christmastide."

"Better a diet of herbs and peace and contentment," retorted Mistress Soames piously.

"Are you sickly, too, Mary?" asked Libby glancing up.

"A—a little," replied Mary hastily. "Perhaps it was the fish, or indeed, even more likely, the excitement."

"Or perhaps the Lord is smiling upon you finally, and you are about to produce the heir, it is your duty to secure, for Sir Edward," suggested Mistress Soames with an unloving smile.

Mary blushed. "I hardly think that likely after all this time," she said uncertainly.

"The Lord blessed Sarah after twenty years, and Elizabeth after even more," replied Mistress Soames. "I myself suffered twelve years disappointment before the Lord blessed me with my son—Oh, Mistress Bess, if we are to talk of slug-a-beds" she added as Bess, pale as the lace at her throat, came down the stairs into the hall.

"Good morrow, Merry Christmas," stammered Bess. "Have you seen the snow?"

"Yes, and felt its effect, too," replied Mary as she reached out a hand to her sister and drew her to the bench. "I must remember to tell Humphrey to tend the fires well today, or we'll all end up with head colds. What can we tempt you to eat for Christmas breakfast, Bess?"

"A little of that bread and milk looks good, young Harry," said Bess, smiling at the little boy's milky face. She glanced anxiously to his mother. "Are you well, Libby?"

Libby's tense face relaxed into a ghost of a smile. "Not so very well, thank you, Bess, but I shall do. And you, does this Christmas morn find you joyful?"

"Oh, it does!" she replied simply, "In spite of everything—all the trouble—" she broke off, as Mistress Soames looked at her with disapproval, "—the snow and everything. I am joyful."

"As, indeed, we all should be, on this the Lord's special day," said Mistress Soames with a sniff. "It is only fitting all should attend divine service, to give thanks for God's greatest gift of all, His son, the Prince of Peace."

"Indeed," agreed Mary, "it is planned we should all attend the eleven o'clock service. I only trust Sir Edward is finally from his bed by then, as he is to read a lesson." She sighed and glanced anxiously at the window. "I doubt any will get to evensong, for the sky appears full of snow." A smile lit her face as Guy Armstrong, accompanied by his sisters, came into the hall. "In fact, with luck, we'll all be snowed in, and will have to keep Christmas up until Easter."

♣

Meanwhile, up in the top chamber of the tower, Hal and Justin faced each other. The cold light of the snow mercilessly picked out the shadows under Hal's eyes, and the tension of Justin's neck muscles.

"So," said Ned, into the lengthy silence which had followed Guy Armstrong's reluctant departure. "Shall we not discuss this matter, like rational human beings?"

"It is my desire to do so," said Justin. "Although, first, I'd like to make it clear how sorry I am for tricking you both. It was not something I did lightly. I could see no clear alternative, which didn't entail misery for Bess and I, so I had little choice."

Ned cast his stern-faced brother an uneasy glance. "Yes, well, naturally, I can appreciate your point of view. Although, as Bess's brother I suppose I should condemn

your actions." He paused glancing again to Hal, waiting for him to speak, and was finally forced to say, "Hal,
have you no comment to make?"

"I said all I am going to say last night," he replied
coldly. "You forced this meeting, Ned, run it your way."

Ned was forced to bite his tongue. If Hal were to
take this stand, the whole affair would become public
knowledge in no time. As Ned saw it, it was essential
none knew of his sister's marriage until they were ready
to tell them, and he was prepared to attack Hal at his
most vulnerable. "What does Libby think of your in-
transigent attitude, Hal?" he asked sharply. "She is
pleased, is she, at the thought of you taking her brother
to law?"

Hal's jaw tightened. "Libby is my wife," he replied
curtly. "She agrees with me in everything."

"I've never heard such nonsense," cried Justin, stung
by this patent lie. "Libby has never, however besotted
she may be, been your cipher."

"So basically, Hal, you see it like this," continued
Ned mercilessly, "you'll not unbend, and agree to this
'fait accompli' as we finally must. We know in our hearts
that our father was actually wrong anyway, but you will
hold out. You'll pretend you've such a high moral tone
and principles, or is it, maybe, just plain spite, mas-

querading under those fine-sounding names? Either way, you'll ruin not only the happiness of two, who are surely dear to you, but also the prospect of peace this Christmas."

Hal cast his outspoken younger bother a look of pained reproach. "I don't know what I've done to earn such disloyalty from you, Ned, but to me it is a matter of principle. And, call me what you will, I shall adhere to my principles."

"I see it as a matter of expediency," said Justin. "I could not afford principles, not when I saw another of your father's daughters was about to be allied for his best interest, but her ultimate unhappiness. As I saw the case, I had no choice, but to act."

"Well, I see it merely as a matter of getting through these next few days, or even longer," said Ned impatiently. "A curse on you both, with your high-flown principles, and fine sounding words. We are faced here with what is a very human dilemma, and one, which will not go away. For the love of God, put aside your squabbling, and let us discuss, in words simple and plain, how we are to prevent Sir Edward, and those chap-fallen boobies he calls kin, poking their noses into this."

"It is simply accomplished," snapped Hal, "when we take our leave after church."

"Talk sense, do!" rejoined Ned. "Take a small child, a pregnant woman and a weeping bride out into two foot of snow, midway through one of the shortest days of the year? It is not a journey I'd care to contemplate."

Justin hid a smile at the truth of this, saying starkly, "Aye, but the same doesn't apply to a lone rider. It's plain I must be the one to leave."

"It will cause much comment if you leave so soon," said Ned, as Hal brightened at the thought. "And to go in such dreadful weather. Have you seen the drifts the other side of the gatehouse? Well, to my mind, it would set up exactly the sort of speculation, taken as it would be, with the tears of Libby and Bess, that we are so anxious to avoid."

"What do you suggest then?" asked Hal bitterly. "You seem suddenly to be blessed with a much clearer understanding than everybody else, so what would you have us do?"

"To my mind we have no choice, but to continue to behave as if nothing has happened. A coldness exists between you and Justin. Should it be commented upon, surely Mary can ascribe it to the jealously, which is most probably its true source," replied Ned brutally, annoyed by Hal's attitude.

Hal's jaw set grimly at this. He glanced away from

his brother's condemning face, looking out over the landscape through the chamber's window. Whiteness blanketed as far as the eye could see, interspersed only with grey belts of woodland, and the snow-clad hills, which stretched as far as Westwood. Behind them, sat banks of clouds, heavy with the yellow-grey light which betokens further falls of snow. He had to admit, Ned was right. There was no way a sane man would contemplate taking a family out in such awful conditions. No more could he, in truth, subject Justin to it.

"Then, I see I have no choice," he said harshly. "If I thought my wishes or words would be heeded, I'd demand you have no further contact with my sister, Justin, but I'll not waste my breath on you. For 'tis plain you'll no more listen to me in this, than anything else."

"No, I'll never allow you to part me from my legally-wedded wife," snapped Justin, in anger, furious at the cutting, bitter words he'd used.

Hal turned angrily on Ned, "You do realise, we'll probably loose the case over this, don't you?"

"A damned good thing, too, as you'd be the first to admit, if you weren't in such a sulk," returned Ned with no sign of repentance. "The very idea of going to law over such a thing is stupid in the extreme."

Hal shrugged, his anger settling into a sullen resentment, that Ned should stand against him. "Then, I have no more to say in the matter," he snapped. "I'll leave it in you capable hands. Now, if you'll excuse me, I promised Harry we could play before church."

Ned grimaced at Justin, as Hal went swiftly from the chamber. "Oh, well, what would Christmas be if one member of a family wasn't in a tantrum over something? Don't fret, Justin. He'll come round by Twelfth Night."

"Twelfth Night?" cried Justin. "Sweet Jesus, I can see it's going to be a very long day."

Chapter Ten

Cecily stood before the fire in the Great Hall, her eyes on the embers of the Yule log, her thoughts far away. She wondered quite how she could contrive, without seeming immodest, to sit beside Ned Westwood at the coming feast. Fanny's warning, as they had struggled back through the snow from church, had been nothing, if not timely. She now knew she wasn't to appear to pay too much attention to a young gentleman, if she wished to successfully secure his affections. The only trouble was that she wished to be near Ned. She liked to listen to the few words he uttered, and she longed to gaze upon his cheerful, freckled face.

"Cecily, ah, I am so glad you are already come," said Mary as she came in bearing a handsome, silver bowl. "For now, you may, if you will, help me brew the drink they call 'the lamb's wool' for the wassail."

"Oh, yes, I should like to do that," replied Cecily eagerly. She had greatly admired Lady Jolyon for many a day, thinking her most beautiful, but now, knowing Ned, wanted to know her even more. She came to join Mary at the table, as Meg and several man-servants followed, bearing a barrel, several bottles of wine, a large cauldron and boxes of various spices.

"Yes, put the spices there, Meg. Andrew, put the cauldron over the fire and fill it with ale. Do you know the local recipe for the wassail, Cecily? No?" she said, as the girl shook her head. "To every quart of good ale," she chanted, as if repeating a rhyme. "Add a bottle of fine white wine and heat both well together. Before they simmer, add the cinnamon, a little grated nutmeg, honey and a handful of roasted crab apples. Then, of course, comes the secret ingredient. This is the one which shall give us all our heart's desire within the year!" Mary laughed gaily and pushed across the dish of withered crab apples. "Will you toast those on a shovel for me? No, prick them well first, with the bodkin, my dear, or they'll burst asunder. Meg, run back to the kitchen. You've forgotten the cinnamon. Yes, that should do, Dicken. You may all go back to the kitchen and prepare another brew for later, but mark this, if you are found so much as tipsy, your master shall hear of it! Oh, and tell Meg to bring the wooden bowls, too. I don't know what possesses that girl. She has no memory at all."

Mary smiled at Cecily, who had glanced up from her apples. "I know traditionally everyone is supposed to sup from the same bowl, indeed Sir Edward may do, so if he chooses. However, I refuse to raise a bowl to my lips, which a churl has slobbered over previously. Here, take my keys, sweetheart, and put out the handsome silver goblets, which are hardly ever used, from the court cupboard, and the ladle to match the bowl. We'll take our wassail in fine style this year." She handed Cecily a set of keys, which hung by a long chain from her waistband.

"Shall I not fetch more napkins, too? For we'll burn our fingers, if the goblets are filled with hot ale, won't we?" asked Cecily, as she inserted the key in the handsome, carved cupboard, which stood against the far wall.

"Yes, of course, an excellent idea," replied Mary. "Oh, Meg, at last. Put down the spice beside the bowl. Mistress Cecily will add it when she's finished the apples, and hasten to the linen closet for another dozen finest linen napkins." She smiled once again in a conspiratorial manner, as Cecily came back to squat beside her, where she was stirring the cauldron, and began to tentatively turn the slowly browning apples. "Mmmm, don't they smell good! You'd not think they'd taste so sour. Can you pass me that jar of honey? No, stay, come take this spoon and stir, whilst I grate the nutmeg, for 'tis so valuable, I dare not trust it to Meg."

Cecily did as her hostess bid her, and Mary bent over the cauldron with her precious nutmeg and a tiny silver grater. "So," she continued, "what think you of my brother?"

"Mr Westwood, ma'am?" asked Cecily innocently.

"No, not Hal, Ned!" replied Mary laughing.

"Oh, Master Ned, he seems most amiable," said Cecily, although she was unable to keep from blushing, as she remembered her sister's warning.

"Which is more than can be said for Hal," murmured Mary, half to herself. For, although Hal had been one of the party, which had ploughed through the snow to church, he'd vouchsafed no word to any, either going thither or coming hence. "So, Ned appears amiable, which indeed he is, to my knowledge. Yes, and he's a good huntsman, too, I daresay, but what did you think of him?"

"I?" Cecily blushed more, and was glad of an excuse to lean over the cauldron to hide her flaming cheeks. "I, I cannot say. Should I add these apples now, ma'am? They are quite done."

"Yes, do that, whilst I count out the cinnamon," agreed Mary. "So, you'll not advance an opinion then?

Yet, Ned was full of questions of you on the way back from church, and sings your praises."

"Mine?" Cecily looked up, her eyes glittering like stars. "Truly, my lady?"

"Yes, truly," replied Mary, laughing as she added the spices. "Now, do pay attention and keep stirring the pot, or the brew will boil and be spoiled. Ah, now, that is splendid. Now I know it's Christmas, only smell that," she inhaled the fragrantly spiced aroma deeply, "now for the final secret ingredient!" She laughed again, a little consciously, as she took a small linen bag from her bodice and emptied the contents, which looked to Cecily like small black seeds, into the simmering brew, while Cecily whisked it round. "Wish, Cecily, wish for your heart's desire, and it shall be granted!" she commanded. Obediently, Cecily closed her eyes and wished with all her heart.

"Come then, let me finish the stirring, whilst you toast the last apples," said Mary, carefully pulling the cauldron from the heat to the edge of the fire. "For I see it wants but a quarter of an hour to three o'clock, when we must all sit down to the feast. Hark, is that not the sound of the wassailers arriving early? Meg, run tell your master his people are come!"

❖

It was a good while later that Cecily sat back in her seat, hemmed in, as usual, between Guy and Fanny. She looked about her. The huge, old table was a mess with broken meats, the carcasses of the goose and sundry fowl, the much-carved side of beef and the dilapidated boar's head bearing witness, along with empty jugs of wine, to how well they had feasted.

Her head was spinning a little, for she was unaccustomed to wine, but had drunk deeply because of the heat from the fire. She laughed helplessly at the play being performed by the mummers in the area in front of the fire.

St George, who was the village blacksmith, in a rusted helm of Puritan mode, and a pair of rubbed leather gauntlets, demonstrated in mime how he had slaughtered the mighty dragon, now sprawled akimbo before the hearth. St George then indicated he hoped to wed the King of Egypt's daughter, who was played by one of the choristers from the morning service, complete with a wig of straw plaits. He displayed a bashful playfulness, which his angelic voice and bearing had given no clue to earlier.

Then, as the mime came to its chaotic close, with St George receiving a buffet on the ear, rather than the desired kiss, that disconsolate knight, amid wails of laughter, lifted up high the wassailing bowl and carried it to the table crying, "Wassail! Wassail!"

Sir Edward got to his feet with the reply of, "Hail, Wassail!" and grasped the offered bowl between his huge hands, then lifted it to his mouth to drink deeply.

St George, with another cry of "Wassail!" received the bowl back and lifted it to his own lips, but stopped in dismay, as Sir Edward gave a loud cry, and fell back in his chair, clutching his throat.

Consternation spread over the blacksmith's face. He lowered the heavy bowl unsteadily to the table, as Mary and Walter Soames leaned over Sir Edward's chair.

"An apple, perhaps?" cried Mary doubtfully. "Is Sir Edward choking on a crab apple?" Walter Soames made no reply, as Sir Edward gave another cry of agony, jerked up in his chair and kicked the table in anguish. The bowl, from which the village blacksmith had drawn back, ashen faced, tipped and spilt the lamb's-wool onto the polished surface of the table, from whence it dripped to the flagstone floor.

"What is it? A seizure?" asked Hal coming quickly to his sister's side, as she laid trembling hands on her husband's flailing arms. "Are you ill, Sir Edward?" he asked loudly, leaning over the man.

"He—he is dying!" whispered Walter Soames, his pallid face rigid with horror as he looked up aghast at Hal.

"Never!" Guy Armstrong leapt up from his seat. "Depend upon it, he's choked on a bone, or some such thing. Hit him hard between the shoulders, Westwood, to dislodge whatever is stopping his breath!"

As Hal rather doubtfully grasped Sir Edward's arm, meaning to follow these instructions as advised, Sir Edward, his face red and contused, his eyes wildly rolling, gave one last, fearful cry, and slumped forward across the table.

"Sweet Jesus!" whispered the blacksmith. "He's gone. Struck down in his prime! Just like old Maggie said he'd be!"

"Killed by a witch!" hissed the dragon, as the mummers drew together in a frightened huddle, to whisper amongst themselves.

"Is he dead, Hal?" Mary cried out in horror, as Libby held her little son's face to her breast, and Justin reached out to clutch Bess's hand.

"Aye, 'tis so," said Hal softly, as he bent over the body. "Poor man, it was either a seizure, or perhaps he did, indeed, choke on a piece of apple."

"Nay, he were ill-wished!" cried the dragon, shaking in his cracked boots. "Weren't he, lads?" He turned back to his companions for support. "Only last Martinmas he had old, wood-wild Maggie put from her cottage, he did, for being behind with her rent. She cursed him, she did. I heard her, so did we all. Didn't we, lads?"

"Aye, aye," nodded the men. "Said he'd never see a lucky day!"

"Said he'd die screaming for mercy!" muttered one.

"Said he'd never see Christmas!" cried another.

"Aye, said he'd fall with the first snows!" agreed a third.

"That will do!" said Hal, with some authority, knowing well how such tales grew out of all proportion, "It is much more likely this is a simple accident." Hal tried hard to bring rational calm to an atmosphere, which was suddenly tense and full of evil.

Sir Edward's dog, which had been crouched at his feet, had taken a good few kicks from the dying man. The poor beast was used to such treatment and merely cowered near the edge of the table, but as Hal picked up a napkin and thoughtfully covered Sir Edward's livid face, the dog inched forward, and began to lap at the spiced wine, which had formed a considerable pool on the floor.

"Libby, take young Harry to the parlour," commanded Hal, as Bess came to slip a comforting arm about Mary's shaking shoulders. "Ned, escort Mistress

Armstrong and her sister there also." Hal broke off, turning to stare in horror, as the poor hound gave a startled yelp of pain, and began to cough. The dog took a few staggering steps into the centre of the hall, before falling on its side in convulsions. All stood, seeming petrified by the sight, Libby in the act of ushering the little boy across the room.

"The dog be dead, too!" cried the blacksmith. "It lapped up the wassail and fell down dead." He raised his huge hand, visibly shaking to his own bloodless lips. "I had it that close to my own mouth!"

"Poisoned!" cried Hal in horror, "Dear God, no."

"Nay, it cannot be," cried Walter Soames looking ghastly. "It—it must be a coincidence. This is my cousin's dog, and much attached to him—perhaps his heart is broken!"

"The poor creature lived in daily fear of him!" cried Mary, her voice ringing harshly in the deathly silence.

"Nay, there are many instances of such devotion," babbled Sir Walter, as little Harry looked curiously at the still animal and asked, "Doggie, Mother?"

"Libby, take the child away," commanded Hal.

Guy Armstrong looked from Mary's ravaged coun-tenance, to the equally shocked faces of his sisters, and was finally galvanised into action.

"Sir Walter, pray escort your poor wife to the parlour," he said, seeing in horror, that Mistress Soames appeared to be smiling. "Indeed, Ned, be a good lad, and help Sir Walter get all the ladies from this dreadful sight!"

"Sir Walter!" cried Hal, suddenly struck that Walter Soames had inherited the lordship Sidworth Castle. "By heaven," he stopped, meeting Justin's eyes, as plainly, the same thought had occurred to both.

Then, Ned and Guy Armstrong hastened the women of the party away to the parlour, and a servant was dispatched for a new jug of strong wine.

Sir Walter seeing doubt in many faces, cried, "Nay, it cannot be so. He must have had a seizure. His manner of living was such—this is all pure conjecture. Sir Edward cannot have been poisoned."

Hal tapped the rim of the silver bowl with a knife, making it rock a little, so that the fast-cooling contents moved, lapping at the sides. "Would you care to lay a wager on it, Sir Walter?"

"Yes, why, yes!" he cried wildly.

"With your life?" asked Guy as he returned and came to stand at the table, pushing forward one of the handsome silver goblets. "Come, sir, show us how confidant you are that your cousin was not poisoned!"

Sir Walter stared at him for a few seconds, beads of perspiration starting from his brow, and then he sank to a stool, shaking his head wordlessly.

"Quo bono?" asked Justin. He came to stand beside Hal looking down at the sprawled body of the dead man.

"Yes," said Hal. "Quite. Who benefits?"

"It wasn't me!" The words were wrenched from Sir Walter, as he saw where this was leading. "I know nothing of it," he added, a haunted look in his eyes.

Chapter Eleven

A while later Ned came back into the Great Hall in time to see Cecily hesitate in the doorway, "Is anything amiss, Mistress Cecily?"

Her hands were clasped tightly to her breast, her eyes huge in her pale face. "No—no," she replied uncertainly, but her gaze travelled to the table, at which they'd all recently sat, and to the white cloth, which covered the dead body. "It—it is only that—Fanny, my sister, wanted something from her chamber. You see, Lady Jolyon is a little faint, with the shock, I expect, so I said I'd run and fetch—but—but now—"

"Now you don't care to cross the hall in the half light, past the corpse?" he suggested.

"I thought the men would still be here," she confessed, "so when I suddenly saw it there, in the dimness—" she broke off, shuddering convulsively.

"In fact, St George, the blacksmith, who is also the village constable, is standing guard in the gloom. But you're right, it grows quite dark. I'll call for some more lights. In the meantime, might I be allowed to run your errand?"

"I don't think Fanny would care for any other to search through her travelling chest, but if you would be so good as to go with me?" she suggested, a little amazed at her own daring.

"It would be a pleasure," he replied, and mentally grimaced as he realised, how like Hal he sounded. He remembered how, in past times, he'd vowed he'd never pay court to a female in such a fashion. His was to have been a stern wooing, with no sweet words, pretty gestures, more a strict understanding between two people of sense; Yet somehow, when confronted by this pretty, helpless girl, soft words and gentleness seemed, not only fitting, but totally right. "Will you wait one moment only, whilst I call for more candles?"

"Simpkin be a-coming, young master, if you're wanting to go with the little lady," observed the constable, from his inglenook.

"Oh, yes, so he is, thank you. Simpkin, bring more candles, if you please. Light the hall well. Be rid of this gloom."

"Lighting the hall won't make no difference," muttered Simpkin. "'Tis evil about, that's what, evil! They say the spirits of those murdered do walk in the night."

"That will do," said Ned sharply. "Light a candle for me. Bring a dozen more to light the hall, and hold your tongue." Ned took the battered candlestick, and offered the wide-eyed Cecily his arm, taking her hand gently, but firmly. He clasped her cold fingers as he compelled her to walk forward, shielding her with his body from the sight of the ominous mound under the tablecloth.

"I know I am being foolish," she confided, as they began to ascend the stairs, "but with Lady Jolyon saying the ghost of Sidworth walks in the gallery, I was suddenly so afraid." She smiled uncertainly. "I expect I am being very foolish, and I am sorry to be such a trouble to you, for I know you are very busy."

"It is no trouble at all," he replied warmly, "but a pleasure to serve you."

"I hadn't thought I would be so very silly," she continued in her innocent way. "I must confess, the sight of the body made me begin to shake."

"Don't dwell upon it," he said in a soothing manner. He could feel her hands fluttering under his and it made him suddenly want to protect her from all ills. "It was a most disturbing sight. I don't think any of us, however wise, or brave, have not been distressed by it."

"Especially when the poor, dear dog went over like that," she whispered.

He could feel how she shuddered. "No, think of something else," he said gently as they reached the gallery.

"I don't seem able to," she confessed, her lips quivering. "It seems to be going round and round in my head and I don't seem able to—" She broke off suddenly with a shriek, as a door banged somewhere below. "Oh! Oh! What was that?"

His arm came about her waist, holding her tight. "Nothing, nothing," he soothed. "No more than a door caught by the wind, I expect."

Tears filled her eyes. "Oh, I am sorry," she whispered weakly. "I am being very foolish."

He smiled down at her. "No, you're not. You're adorable," he replied and bent his head to kiss her. Amazement held her perfectly still for a few seconds, then her hands grasped the velvet of his coat, and she returned his kiss with all her heart.

"Now it is my turn to be sorry," he said as he released her with a rueful smile, "I shouldn't have done that." He paused to light a candle from the one he carried.

"Why?" she asked breathlessly, her eyes shining as she gazed up into his face.

"Because I am taking advantage of you, of your fears, of your youth," he said, but his eyes never left her flower-like face.

"I—I don't mind," she blushed prettily.

He laughed and kissed the tip of her nose lightly. "Oh, you are adorable," he said unsteadily brushing her rosy cheek again, seeking her soft lips. "No, this won't do," he released her again and tucked her hand back through is arm, directing their steps along the gallery. "We go on your sister's errand, Mistress Cecily."

"So we do," she agreed, biting her bottom lip and wondering if her too-free behaviour had disgusted him, and led to a sudden change of heart.

Timidly, she raised her eyes to his face as they proceeded along the gallery, and found that a glance could convey as much as a kiss.

"I must seek out your brother immediately," said Ned, plainly following his own train of thought. "He is your guardian?"

"Oh yes," she replied, "but I have to tell you plainly, I have no dowry. Guy is struggling to even find the money to marry Fanny decently."

"I don't give a groat for that," he said grandly, only recollecting as the words left his lips, that his father most certainly would. Then he thought of Hal, and realised that it was essential he get him to view the match with favour.

"This is our chamber," announced Cecily, coming to a halt.

"Should you like me to remain here?" he suggested delicately.

"No, I would like you to stay with me, but I fear I sound immodest saying so," she said honestly.

"I think, under such circumstances it will be allowed," he replied, a laugh in his voice. "Especially if we leave the door wide open." He did so, lighting a candle for her and accompanying her to the large, iron-banded travelling chest, which was at the foot of the bed.

"You sleep here, with your sister?" he asked, his eyes straying in the gloom to the bed, with its coverlet of threadbare silk.

She glanced up from where she knelt before the chest, neatly and deftly turning back the contents, so as not to muddle them, and blushed once again. "Yes, yes," she stammered, confused by the intensity of his gaze.

"Then I shall know whence to direct my thoughts of you this night. I shall surely dream of your sweet face, and be secure in the knowledge you, at least, need not be troubled by bad dreams, safe beside your sister."

She looked up again, her eyes bright, but with a flustered air. "I— I rather think you have effectively banished all dreadful thoughts from my mind," she said artlessly. "My head is now filled by delightful dreams."

Once again, his smile was a caress. "Don't look at me like that," he commanded, his voice unsteady. "I'm resolved not to kiss you again, until I've spoken with both your brother and mine."

She rose to her feet, Fanny's box found and tucked under her arm. "I would not have you break any resolve you are determined to keep on my account," she said demurely.

"Oh, Cecily, don't tempt me," he said, with a shaky laugh. "I should not even be speaking to you like this, without your brother's consent."

She peeped up at him from beneath her eyelashes shyly. "I don't greatly care about Guy's consent," she murmured provocatively. "As long as you have mine, you need have no fear."

He shook his head, his eyes glowing with love. "No, 'tis not honourable. Hal would say it is not honourable."

"Hal? Pooh! He is so stiff, so cold, so formal. I should not care to have such as he for my lover."

"But, Hal is handsome, polished, elegant—he says just exactly what he always should," protested Ned, shocked by her words. "Hal is everyone's ideal."

"Not mine," she replied firmly. "He's—he's too hand-some—too perfect and ready with the polished phrase. Even his courtesy is just a little weary, to my mind. I like a man to have fire in him. A man, who may have faults, yes, but is human."

Ned laughed at that. "Oh, Hal is human, believe me, and has faults enough like the next man. And, if it's fire you are wanting, you should see him in a temper." He sighed at the thought. "Aye, that's something I don't want disturbed. So, if you have your sister's box, we'll return to the parlour."

She walked past him to the door, her head down-cast, but paused there whilst he doused the light and came to shut the door after them. Then she stood on tiptoe to press a kiss firmly on his cheek. "There now, if you cannot kiss me, for the sake of your honour, I'll kiss you."

He raised his fingers to his cheek and was rather amazed by the wash of emotions he felt, his last resent-ment at being much like other men, fading fast. If this was love, what a fool he'd been to vow abjurance of it. No wonder it altered men so. What did it matter if he appeared a fool? Better, surely, to be a happy fool in paradise, than a wise man in a desert.

"Cecily, you are a little hussy, and I adore you," he

said warmly, "Now come, back to the parlour and your sister's eye."

✤

Justin looked for the opportunity to have a few words with Hal as everyone, as if by consent, gathered by the fire in the parlour, leaving Sir Edward in solitary state in his hall.

In the parlour, emotions were still running high. Mary sat on the seat by the window, her face as pale as the snowy landscape beyond, her fingers clenched about the goblet of wine Guy Armstrong had pressed upon her. Bess sat protectively beside her, and Mistress Soames a little to her left. It was the latter's scrutiny, which caused the tears to slip down Mary's cheeks unchecked, for there was no kindness in her eyes, only judgement.

"It is difficult to know what to do for the best," Hal was saying. "The constable says it is ten miles to Helchester and it isn't likely the sheriff would be there today. I don't want to put myself forward, but I have recently been invited to take a place on the Bench in my own county, and in these distressing circumstances—"

"You're a justice of the peace?" asked Sir Walter. "You are very young, for such an honour."

"The honour is, I think, more in recognition of my father," replied Hal, "and that I continue in my uncle's position."

"There are many young justices since the King came again," remarked Justin blandly. "The need to remove those who supported Cromwell, means that loyal men are pressed into service. Hal works very hard for the good of the county."

"Indeed, it is thanks to Hal, the building has at last begun on the poor house," cried Libby indignantly, looking up from where she was talking quietly to her distressed child.

"How you all rush to his defence," sneered Geoffrey Soames. "He is indeed the pet lamb, Sir Edward called him."

"He is a whitened sepulchre glistening in the sun," said Avis Soames. "He is—"

"Hush, madam," said her husband hurriedly. "I meant no insult, Mr Westwood. I was merely a little surprised at your youth, but as Mr Danvers suggests, loyalty to the Crown is everything these days."

"Well, I object," said Geoffrey Soames. "I don't give a damn how virtuous he is. He'll not take command here. Why, it is his sister, who is most likely the murderer."

"Unsay that, sir!" cried Hal. "How dare you accuse Lady Jolyon in this fashion, with no reason or proof?"

"Wait, Hal," cried Justin. "Do not fly into a fury. We must, at all events, remain calm. Mr Soames is surely distressed at his cousin's demise. Indeed, we are all shocked by the horror we witnessed."

Hal had time to consider the matter more coolly. "Justin you are correct. We are all shocked and horrified by this unfortunate event, but we must try to achieve some order, some sense. If we are to remain here together, we must try to understand what has occurred."

"My cousin is dead," said Sir Walter heavily, "that is what has occurred."

"You have my sincere commiserations, Sir Walter," replied Hal, "but for the safety and comfort of all, we must try to understand what has occurred. I suggest we ask Mr Danvers, who is a man of law, to ask questions of us, that we might bring some sense to what has happened here."

Chapter Twelve

"I—I must thank you, Hal," said Justin uncertainly, in an aside, as Cecily slipped back into the parlour against the background of Avis Soames's dire predictions of death and despair. "It was very just of you to suggest I take control of the proceedings. I'm glad your opinion of my abilities has survived our quarrel. Although, I guess it cost you dear to recommend me."

"Not at all," replied Hal icily, refusing to unbend. "I know you to be a most unbiased judge in such matters, and to have a very full knowledge of the law. I do not need to approve of your personal conduct." Justin flushed at this and opened his mouth to retort in kind, but Ned, hurrying back in from the errand he'd been originally sent on, interrupted the incipient quarrel.

"The constable, Zac Drew, reports that he has talked to all the servants, and such were the comings and goings for the feast, that almost anyone could have taken the opportunity to poison the wassail bowl."

"Did he?" asked Justin. "Yes, I suspected as much. Well, tell him to come here, if you please, Ned. I think we'd best begin proceedings with a general discussion."

Hal glanced about the dim chamber. Libby was looking anxious, huddled on a settle next to Harry. Mary's ghostly face showed the effects of the shock, as did Bess, who constantly patted her sister's hands, as she tried to comfort her. Avis Soames, still mouthing doom and despair at regular intervals, sat on the other side of the fire. Cecily Armstrong rocked back and forth on a joint stool, at the feet of her sister's embroidery frame, and hugged her knees as she tried to contain her happiness. The men stood about uneasily, uncertain of their role, until Hal suggested they also sat.

"For I rather fear," he added grimly, "we have a long night ahead of us. Mr Danvers, won't you begin? Sir Walter, please take this chair. I'll sit on the window seat with Lady Jolyon."

Justin took his place behind the table laid out with paper, pen and an inkwell. "Lady Jolyon, perhaps you could begin by telling us about the brewing of the wassail ale," he said politely.

"I made it to the same recipe as I have every year," said Mary quietly. "It was one Sir Edward's grandmother wrote down. It's called 'lamb's-wool' locally, for 'tis so soft. The recipe must be forty, or fifty years old. I made it exactly as I did last year, and the year before. I brewed it in the cauldron over the fire, from ingredients taken from the kitchen."

"Did any see you mix it?" Justin asked, making notes as she spoke.

"Yes, any who came through the hall. The servants, who brought the wine and ale; my wench, Meg, who brought the goblets and napkins; and Mistress Cecily, who helped mix the brew," replied Mary, her voice unsteady.

"Mistress Cecily?" Justin asked, and smiled, as she looked up, startled. "You saw the making of the punch, did you?"

"Yes sir," she replied quickly. "I was there the whole time. I roasted the apples."

"You saw all that Lady Jolyon did? Everything that went into the bowl?" he asked keenly.

"Oh yes, for it was all gathered ready. The ale, the wine, the honey and apples; the men brought in the herbs and spices—all except the secret ingredient," she added smiling a little, as she realised how effective it had been in giving her her heart's desire.

"Secret ingredient?" Justin repeated the words in a surprised voice. "And what exactly was the secret ingredient, if you please, Lady Jolyon?"

"Nothing, nothing of any significance," stammered Mary, suddenly even paler, as Hal glanced to her in concern, "merely a few more herbs, that is all."

"A few herbs?" queried Justin, not caring for her unease.

She hesitated, going first red in the face, and then so pale again, she looked as if she were about to faint. "It was a mere foolishness, Mr Danvers, nothing but a potion for—for good luck—that my wench got for me."

"A potion, Mary?" asked Hal sharply. He was anxious she should explain more clearly, for it sounded highly dubious to his trained ears. "For heaven's sake, what folly is this? You make it all sound like a green-sick wench, procuring a love potion."

Mary's cheek stained crimson at the biting contempt in his voice. "So it was," she said, her voice very low. "A potion to bring one their heart's desire. Meg fetched it for me, from the witch over at Henbury."

"Have no truck with witches, they are the devil's creatures!" said Avis Soames.

"What was in the potion, ma'am?" asked Justin patiently, as Hal exclaimed in exasperation.

"I—I do not know exactly," she replied, "but I know it was harmless. She swore it was harmless."

"Harmless, or not, it gave you what you wanted, didn't it?" Geoffrey Soames remarked, a nasty glint in his eye. "Why should you care what it contained? You knew my cousin would be the first to drink, and that his death would set you free."

"No!" she cried in horror. "No, it wasn't like that. I didn't want Sir Edward dead! I tell you, Meg said the old woman swore it would harm no one!"

"But how else could you achieve your heart's desire, unless Edward were to die?" asked Sir Walter slowly. "There was no other way you could be free from his brutality, unless by his death."

"And you must be free, must you not, my lady?" Avis Soames said, her thin face suddenly filled with venom. "You did need, most urgently, to be rid of your husband, did you not? For I think once Sir Edward discovered your shame, he'd have put you and your bastard out. The Lord says all adulteresses shall be cast out, not contaminate those who love and fear His word."

"Madam," protested Justin, his glance going to Cecily, who was staring about her in dismay. "I must beg you to moderate your words and tone. You cannot cast aspirations on another's character in this manner without proof."

"Proof?" sneered Geoffrey Soames. "What proof is needed, has not her behaviour been proof enough? Do you not think the whole county doesn't know of it, and will know within hours, how Sir Edward lies conveniently dead, whilst his wife is pregnant with another man's child?"

"Dear God, Mary, is this true?" cried Hal, aghast, as all eyes turned on his sister.

Mary bowed her head in shame. "Yes, I am with child," she admitted in a whisper, as Bess squeezed her hand in an effort to give her comfort. "But even so, I never intended my husband any harm. As God is my witness, I put nothing in that punch I would not happily have drunk myself."

"Did—did Sir Edward know of your infidelity?" asked Hal, stumbling over the words, his brow thunderous.

"No," she admitted, reluctantly.

"He must have been the only one that didn't then," sneered Geoffrey Soames.

"It—it was my intention to—to leave Sidworth at once, after Twelfth Night," she whispered. "I would have gone as soon as I was sure, but I did not think Sir Edward would have thanked me for abandoning my duties as chatelaine, and leaving him with all the preparations for Christmastide." She glanced up to meet Hal's flinty, disapproving face. "Don't look at me like that, Hal. I know I have sinned greatly, but I am no murderess."

"An adulteress sounds little better to my ear," he snapped curtly.

"That's enough, Westwood," interrupted Guy Armstrong, who'd been growing grim. "Lady Jolyon has admitted her fault. There need be no further discussion here, of matters which concern none, but her and myself." His cold glance swept to Justin, "May I suggest we send for the wench, Meg? She can, most surely, confirm her mistress's story."

"Or is just as likely in her pay," snapped Geoffrey Soames.

"I really must request you to hold your tongue, Mr Soames," said Justin coldly. "I have been asked to look into this affair, and I will do so in my own way, drawing my own conclusions. I cannot but be aware, that you are most anxious to exonerate your father and yourself, but your constant interruptions are of little help, and I need not reminded you, there is such a thing as slander."

A very uncomfortable silence fell, as they waited for the serving wench. Geoffrey opened his mouth to speak, but was silenced by a shake of the head from his father.

None cared to catch the eye of another. Libby came and slipped her arm about the waist of the weeping Mary, and hugged her by way of expressing her sympathy, totally ignoring Hal's glare as he was forced to move.

Ned sank to the floor next to Hal in amazement. His young face was suddenly very serious as he understood the implications, and he began to wonder what effect this would have on his own affairs. He stole a look at Cecily, wondering what she made of it all, and if she was as shocked as he, but Cecily sat with her eyes downcast, to hide her tears.

Of course, she'd known Guy admired Lady Jolyon. He'd not troubled to conceal it, but to be her lover? For her to be carrying his child, and deceiving her husband, well it was the most shocking thing she ever heard. And, what was more, she'd be an aunt. Under the feeling of shock, a glimmer of pleasure rose as she thought of the baby. Lady Jolyon, a murderess, like Lady Macbeth? The idea was laughable, only no one was laughing. Something was amiss here; it was all very wrong. Tears spilled over as she realised her foolish words had brought one she admired to such a perilous pass.

"Ah!" Justin looked up from where he'd been making copious notes, as the slatternly figure of Meg appeared in the doorway. "Meg, come in, girl. We have questions to ask you."

"Sir," she dropped a reluctant curtsey and glanced about the chamber, as she advanced a few steps with a knowing, complacent air.

"It's about the potion you fetched for me from the old, wise woman at Henbury, Meg," said Mary frowning a little at the oddly sly, triumphant, look on the girl's face.

"Oh, the love philtre you were so desperate for, you mean? The one to keep hold of your lover, Mistress?" she asked insolently.

"No," said Mary sharply, "The one you told me of, the potion, which gave one their heart's desire!"

"'Tis the same thing," said the girl pertly.

"What it was obtained for, matters not," said Hal, impatient with Justin for allowing the wench the opportunity to be impudent. "Did you fetch it for my sister, or not?"

The wench fluttered her lashes at Hal, whose good looks had impressed her, even as his cold manners had intrigued her. "Oh, aye, sir," she said soulfully, "I goes out of my way to oblige her ladyship."

"What instructions did this old woman give you?" asked Justin sharply.

She reluctantly turned her limpid gaze back to Justin. "I don't rightly recall, sir," she added, with enough hesitation to make it an insult.

"Don't play the fool, wench," said Hal severely, knowing that, given the slightest leeway, she'd delight in telling all manner of lies. "Answer Mr Danvers immediately. What did this witch say? What was her name, by the way? Was she the same woman who cursed Sir Edward earlier in the year?"

"No, sir," said the constable from his place by the door, "That were Maggie Smith from the village, it were. This witch is Sib Thornton from Henbury Copse."

"You appear to suffer a surfeit of local witches," remarked Hal, coldly.

"I dare say the term is a loose one, and they are little more than old, wise-women," replied Justin.

"Indeed, Mistress Thornton does no harm," said Mary quickly. "She is renown locally for her skill with herbs. Many, aye, and the gentry too, consult her in sickness. Sir Edward often did, about his horses."

Justin, noting the constable's sceptical look, had his doubts, but Hal was anxious to return to the point at issue and said, "What were the instructions this, so called, wise-woman gave you, wench? Answer Mr

Danvers at once."

"Well, sir," she turned back to Hal, casting him a side long, flirtatious look. "She said as how it were to be brewed in a loving cup, or added to a punch, and that if the one as made the punch made the wish, they'd get their heart's desire, whatever that be. 'Tis a common enough philtre, your honour. I could get one for you, if you wish it."

Hal returned the look icily. "I do not wish it," he replied curtly. "I already have my heart's desire."

"Well, if you be sure," she replied, with the return of her former insolence.

"I am very sure, and equally sure that you'd do well to keep away from witches, or even wise women," he returned sharply. "Indeed, if you were a servant of mine I'd have you beaten until you knew how to conduct yourself."

"If I were a servant of thine, I'd know just how to conduct myself," she returned pertly, with a sway of her hips.

"That will do, Meg, you may go," cried Mary, who was scandalised enough by the girl's loose behaviour to be roused from her despair.

"I ain't ready to go yet. I've summat of my own to say," returned Meg defiantly, setting her hands on her hips. She glanced around, certain of their shocked attention. "It be this: Sir Edward and me, we were lovers. And I have his brat here," she slapped her flat stomach.

"Lovers?" Mary gasped in amazement.

"Aye, just because he weren't to your taste, my lady, didn't mean he couldn't satisfy no woman," she sneered. "Happen he like a wench, with a bit of life in her, and not a stone statue."

"That's enough," said Justin, as the shock of her words echoed about the crowded chamber. "You were told to leave. Do so at once, or I'll have you put out."

"Nay, then," she snapped her eyes flashing, "if this be a boy, he's heir to all this!" she waved a reddened, grimy hand. "I've a right to stay."

"Had you been legally married, which wasn't possible, as Sir Edward was already wed to your mistress, you perhaps could have a claim upon the estate—if you had been able to produce proof of Sir Edward's paternity," returned Justin, with solemn authority. "But, as you cannot do either of these things, I'm afraid you are nothing but an impudent strumpet, caught with a bastard. Now, leave this chamber, as your mistress bids you."

"I can prove he were my lover," she cried angrily, "Everyone knew, but her."

"I have no doubt you were one of the many trollops Sir Edward kept, and that it was common knowledge," said Justin cuttingly, "but you don't have a wedding band upon your finger, so your union was not legal."

"So a bit of gold on a finger, means she's not a trollop, and I am!" cried the girl as she glared at Justin, incensed. He shrugged his shoulders in reply. Only further angered, she made a derisive sound with her lips as she flounced to the door. There she paused dramatically, "You, you all think you're so fine and clever sitting here talking. I know who killed Sir Edward, and it weren't my fine, lily-livered mistress!"

Justin frowned after the girl. "Perhaps you should bring her back, Drew," he said thoughtfully. "I don't expect she knows anything but—"

"Oh course, she won't know anything!" snapped Hal, "I've met her sort many times. She lies just for the attention it brings."

"Liars burn in the very pit of hell!" said Avis Soames, her eyes glittering, "as do fornicators and adulteresses. Damnation and eternal torment awaits you all!"

"I have to say, I agree with the wench, Mary," said Hal, ignoring the voice of doom. "There is not one iota of difference between you."

"And I have to say that I'll ram your teeth down your

throat, Westwood, if you direct another remark like that at Mary!" cried Guy Armstrong, losing his patience.

A heated babble of protest and anger broke out, as overcharged emotions and bruised feelings rose to the surface. For a few minutes Hal and Guy Armstrong threw insults back and forth, and very nearly came to blows, whilst Justin struggled to restore order, finally only doing so by banging hard on the table with his fist.

"Silence, all of you!" he cried loudly. "This may not be a court of law, but it's not a drunken brawl, either. Sit down at once, Hal, and hold your tongue. You, of all people, should know better. This is no way to conduct an enquiry." Then, as everyone was brought back to a sense of decorum, and settled back in their seats, he added, "Now, we'll get on one whole lot faster if everyone keeps their opinions and criticisms to a more private occasion, especially you, Hal. You have made it abundantly clear you don't approve of Lady Jolyon's conduct, or indeed, that of any of us, but we'll get to the truth much faster if we stick firmly to the facts."

"Let he who is without sin, cast the first stone," said Libby quietly, into the silence this engendered. Her glance coldly swept her angry husband's face as she cradled the sobbing Mary in her arms. Hal had stiffened at Justin's measured reproof, but at Libby's words, his angry colour faded and he recoiled, almost as if from a physical blow, then sank back against the window to cool his heated brow.

Justin, glancing about the ravaged faces, decided he could achieve little more with them. "Indeed, I don't know that we can discover much more this evening. The ladies grow distressed and weary. It is my suggestion that we all retire and spend sometime in contemplation. It could well be, that one of us, unbeknownst to ourselves, holds the key to this mystery."

"Retire?" Geoffrey Soames voice came sharply. "It is but nine of the clock. Are we to retire and allow the culprit to escape? Is that your plan?"

"It appears to have escaped your notice, Soames, but we are snowed in here," said Justin wearily. "I doubt very much even the strongest of us could make it to the gatehouse."

"The men have returned to the village," cried Sir Walter querulously.

"No, sir, they thought on making an attempt, but decided against it," said Justin. "The snow now being too deep, and the blizzard too great."

"Well, I still object to Lady Jolyon being given the chance to escape," cried Geoffrey Soames. "We've as good as found her guilty, for 'tis plain she was."

"On the contrary, we've done nothing of the sort," said Justin firmly. "And it seems to me, everyone is playing underhand games in this castle."

"Who's to say we won't all be poisoned by the morning? Or smothered in our beds, if she's allowed to go free?" the man continued angrily.

Mary flushed vividly at these cruel words, uttering an inarticulate cry of protest, but Hal intervened. "Quite correct, Soames," he agreed coolly. "I was about to suggest myself, that Mary be locked up for her own safety."

"Safety?" Guy Armstrong queried, disliking the suggestion.

"Yes, somebody is taking great care to implicate my sister, so much so, that I fear, if she is left alone all night, we shall find her lifeless body on the morrow. With a few words written to indicate that her despair and repentance made her take her own life."

"But you would lock me up, Hal?" cried Mary, fearfully.

"It is the safest way, Mary," he replied coldly. "Justin shall lock you in your chamber, and keep possession of the key."

"I shall be locked in with you, Mary, never fear,"

said Libby, seeing how afraid she was.

"No, Libby you are not strong enough, and little Harry might need you," the words were startled from Hal, and uttered before he had time to think.

"I'll stay with her." Bess embraced her frightened sister, but recognised the sense of what Hal said.

"Surely, if there is danger, it should be a man," cried Guy Armstrong. "Lest an attempt be made on her life," —he met Hal's thunderous eyes, adding hastily—"it must be you, Westwood—or your young brother, to remain with Lady Jolyon."

"I shall certainly keep watch all night, outside the door to her chamber," he replied austerely, "but with Bess for company, I cannot see how any further ill could befall her. Well, gentlemen?" Hal turned to Sir Walter and his son, "Do these arrangements satisfy you?"

"I suppose we have little choice," snapped Geoffrey Soames. "It has been plain from the beginning, you would take control of this affair, Westwood, to be sure your sister was exonerated."

"You may be sure, I'll see my sister is not unjustly accused and found guilty," he replied, "but Mr Danvers is in control of the enquiry."

"He's nought but a tame dog, sniffing after another of your family," he sneered. "Don't think I'm such a fool I can't see what's going on. However, it won't snow forever and once there's a thaw, I'll upset this cosy little scheme you've got here. I'll ride for the sheriff and I'll see that trollop, your sister, flung in the darkest prison cell, as she deserves."

"Well—well—he is a little distressed, you know," stammered Sir Walter, as his son flung from the chamber. "I'm sure he doesn't mean—None of us would care to unjustly accuse Lady Jolyon, but the circumstances are such—"

"She is a wicked whore!" cried his wife. "She will burn in the fires of hell eternally. There is no hope for her. She is condemned by her own mouth, to eternal damnation, without relief. Waste no pity on her in this life, but take heed of her end."

"Get that carrion crow out of here," roared Guy Armstrong forcibly, as Mary's sobs increased, "and for God's sake keep a bridle on the tongue of one of your curst family."

"Come, my love," Sir Walter hurried his fanatical wife to the door. "I'll bid you all good night and sweet repose," he muttered hurriedly as he went out.

"Sweet repose? The man's a fool!" cried Guy wrathfully.

"Nay," Justin, laughed reluctantly as he was still stinging from Geoffrey Soames's insults, "A poor soul caught between Sycilla and Charbrys."

"Come, Mary. Come, Bess," commanded Hal. "I'll escort you to your chamber. Mr Danvers, you'll come also, to lock the door?"

"Westwood, be a good fellow, allow me but five minutes with your sister," said Guy Armstrong quickly.

"I think you've done more than enough damage, Armstrong," he replied coldly. "Mary, Libby, come now, if you please." Insistently, he stood at the door, waiting to shepherd his womenfolk from the room, ignoring the resentment of the other two men.

Obediently, the women rose to their feet, wishing those remaining goodnight, and went from the chamber, leaving Armstrong disconsolate, with his sisters and Ned.

Fanny had just started to express her shock and dismay, when Bess hurried back in and said, "Ah, there's my handkerchief. Oh, Mr Armstrong, would you be so good as to accompany Mr Danvers to his chamber presently?"

"If you wish it, ma'am," he said politely.

"I do, sir," she replied, "Goodnight again."

Chapter Thirteen

As the members of the party separated to seek their own chambers, Geoffrey Soames wandered out towards the courtyard and stables. The others may have been shocked and ready to retire for the night, but he wasn't. He was immured in this god-forsaken place by the weather, but, at least, he could find himself some occupation to while away the next few hours.

"Hist!"

He glanced irritably to the screens passage to see the face of the maidservant Meg outlined in the dim light.

"What is it?" he demanded curtly.

"Have they found her guilty? My mistress, Lady Jolyon, I mean," she asked anxiously twisting her hands.

"No, but they will," he replied, then turned back to her, as a thought occurred to him.

"But she didn't do it. She could no more kill, than hurt a fly," cried the girl, half in anger, half in distress. "Sir Edward always called her such a milksop creature that she'd not even answer back. Why, he used to beat her 'til the blood ran, but she never even raised her voice to him, after the first."

"Perhaps the worm finally turned," he replied callously. "Perhaps she'd had enough of his beatings."

"Nay, for he'd not touched her in a twelve month," said the girl impatiently. "He got tired of her. She was a nothing, a poor mouse of a creature, with no fire in her belly, he said."

"As opposed to you, eh? Only you've his brat in your belly," he said with a sneer.

"'Twas the only way to stop the beatings," she replied complacently. "'Tis well known he'd never harm a woman once she was with child."

"Aye, but what would you have done when the nine months was up?" he leered with a grin.

"I am pregnant," she cried. "I'm no fool. Polly tried that one, and when he found out, he beat her so bad, she died of it."

"Poor wench," he replied sarcastically, showing no dismay or concern. "So, what will you do now, Meg?"

"Do?" she asked, frowning up at him, puzzled by the question.

"Well, your master is dead. I don't think your chances of your mistress taking you are high. She'll either go to prison, if I have my way, or, more likely, return home with that brother of hers. He'll certainly do his best to get her off."

"Do you think she'll go with her brother, Mr Westwood?" she asked with interest.

"I think he'll insist she return to his home," he agreed, with another sneer, "but forget that idea. He won't take you. He had your measure at once."

She shrugged her shoulders. "I could bring him round," she said. "He's just forgotten what excitement is, with that wife of his. Did you see her? Why, she's nothing."

"They say he's devoted to her, nevertheless," he replied unpleasantly. "No, as I see it, you'll have to stay here until my mother decides you must be punished as a strumpet."

"I don't have to stay here for her," spat the girl. "I could go back to my own in the village."

"Aye, and they'll welcome you with open arms, no doubt? You and your bastard?" he asked idly. "You got something from my cousin for all your trouble, I take it?"

"No," she replied slowly. "He were going to give me a purse of gold and a pearl necklace, he were, if it were a lad. Not to mention fine gowns and laces."

"All empty promises now," chuckled Geoffrey, with heavy sarcasm. "So you've not even a shilling to sweeten your family, and another mouth to feed."

She was silent for a space, plainly reviewing her situation. Then she added with a tinge of defiance, "I'll get one of the village lads to wed me."

"What? When you've broadcast so far and wide that you're pregnant with Sir Edward's bastard? No man would take you, but that you'd a bag of gold to sweeten him."

He paused, his eyes running over her face and shape. "Of course, you could find another protector."

Her eyes were needle sharp. "Are you offering to become one?"

"I might consider it," he replied coolly. "But of course, you must remember you're damaged goods now. No bags of gold for you, my lady. You'll be thankful for your keep, if you come to me."

"You'll keep your mother away from me?" she asked quickly. "I know her sort, she'd have me stripped and whipped through the village."

"I'll not allow her to do it, although I might care to myself," he replied coolly.

She glanced up to his dark face, her eyes wary. "Like Sir Edward, are you?" she asked with resignation.

"I had never considered it, but you know, it has its attractions," he replied, with an evil grin. "We'll have to see how things develop. In the meantime, you can meet me at midnight in the stables."

"Midnight!" she cried, "Its not yet ten of the clock, and its cold in them stables."

"I've yet to talk to my father," he replied dismissively. "And don't worry, you'll not feel the cold when I've finished with you. Now get gone, or I'll change my mind."

Meanwhile, up in the high, vaulted chamber, which had been Sir Edward's, the new Lady of Sidworth Castle, was in haste to claim her own.

"My dear," said Walter Soames, unease in his voice as he watched his wife efficiently strip all the dead man's personal belongings from the chamber. "Should we even be here? Poor Edward is barely cold. I can't help feeling this shows a sad lack of—well—fitness of things?"

"Don't be a fool, Walter. If nothing else, cold he is. It is freezing in this place. One of your first acts must be to stop up all the draughts and build up decent fires."

"My love," he hesitated, not knowing how to express

himself, and fearing her sharp replies. "Do you not think we should—that is to say—I would rather not take any action—be seen to anticipate my honour—until this—this unpleasantness is resolved."

"Not take any action? That is plain. When do you? Where is Geoffrey?" She looked about her as she spoke, as if she had suddenly noticed his absence. "Did you not tell him we needed to talk?"

"Indeed, I did, my love," Sir Walter said in soothing tones. "And he will be here directly, I have no doubt."

"We must arrange matters," she cried shrilly. "Things cannot go on as they are. Have you not noticed how those Westwood's are taking command? You must assert yourself more, Walter. You are the senior, both in rank, and age. That Hal Westwood, he needs to be put in his place."

"Indeed, my love, you are, as ever, quite correct. I will bring the matter to his attention tomorrow."

"They don't give me my title, have you notice that?" She rounded on him, making him jump. "They still call her, that wicked, brazen hussy, they still call her Lady Jolyon!"

"As indeed she still is, my dear, if only as a courtesy," he said, in soothing accents. "Yes, you are right, however, you must, and shall, be given your correct title. I do not think it was done of malice, more that with the shock of everything, none thought of it."

"They called you Sir Walter at once," she snapped.

"They did, but I think Guy Armstrong did so to call into question my position. I think he, rather than that poor woman, is the murderer, although perhaps she had a guilty foreknowledge, which will surely condemn her.

" No, I think Armstrong had hoped to cast suspicion upon myself, that they might get away with so heinous a crime. Armstrong is an unsteady man, my dear. I wonder that Edward had him at his table. His family were Royalists, you know, and his land and money is sadly depleted. They say he has debts everywhere. Not that they are one of our ancient families, not like the Jolyons. No, Armstrong's uncle won the estate in a game of dice, it seems, and having no heir, the estate came to this fellow, Guy. I have heard it said Armstrong would cut his grandmother's throat for a groat—but that is gossip, and I should not repeat it without foundation.

"We must stick to the facts, as Mr Danvers says, and they are unsavoury enough. I am shocked, I cannot deny, that Lady Jolyon, the dowager Lady Jolyon, should stoop so low as to consort with Armstrong, and horrified that she should be mixed up in this dreadful affair. Only think of the scandal, but then, I am being selfish. What is scandal to poor Edward, poisoned at his own table?"

"I see Hal Westwood is determined to prove his sister innocent, if he can," she replied, by no means appeased by his meanderings.

"Well, that is understandable," said Sir Walter. "I find Hal Westwood a very irritating young man in some ways, but I must confess, I admire his devotion to his family."

Lady Soames sniffed by way of a reply to this pleasantry. "Geoffrey is still not come," she cried impatiently, "I shall go and find him."

"He is a man full-gown, my love," he said watching her uneasily. "Best not to interfere with his concerns."

"You allow him too much freedom," she cried hurrying to the door. "I shall find out exactly what he is at."

♣

Hal saw his sisters locked safely into Mary's bedchamber, and his wife and son tucked up warmly before a good fire in their chamber. He then returned to find Ned, Justin and Guy Armstrong taking a cup of wine together. "Here are the keys, Justin," he said curtly. "I recommend you take them with you to bed, and lock your door, opening it to none. In my haste to keep Mary safe, I've put you in danger, it would seem."

Justin dropped the keys into his pouch. "Don't fret for me," he replied coldly. "I can take care of myself."

"I'll come and keep you company, whilst we discuss this matter of your father's venture," Guy Armstrong made this suggestion, as both got to their feet. "Pass me that jug of wine if you will, young Ned, I've a feeling this is going to be a long night."

"Did you see the Armstrong sisters to their chamber?" Hal asked of his brother, as the other two men went together up the stairs.

"Well, I went along with Armstrong, but he said there was no need for them to lock themselves in. I'm not so sure. I'd sooner they did, if there's a madman about."

"They stand in no danger," soothed Hal.

"What's the plan then, Hal?" asked Ned presently, as Hal sat sipping his wine.

"Plan? I have no plan, as such," he replied. "I was just going to sleep on that settle outside Mary's door. It's at the head of the staircase, not far from the base of the tower. I can watch out for any going to the door, and keep an eye on who goes up the tower."

He hesitated, then added, "If you care to, you could also take up a position in the gallery, close at hand to the Armstrong sisters's chamber, I know they should be safe, but I've a feeling there's trouble abroad tonight."

"Yes, I'll do that," said Ned looking happier. "I agree with you. There is trouble abroad."

Chapter Fourteen

Justin and Guy made themselves comfortable in Justin's chamber.

"I'm sorry to intrude upon you like this, Danvers," said Guy Armstrong, taking the glass of wine Justin offered him. "But that's the message your wife, Bess, gave me, when she returned to collect her handkerchief."

"You were to join me in my chamber," said Justin thoughtfully. "I must confess I cannot for the life of me see why, but I have no objection."

"Perhaps she feared for your life," suggested Guy. "After all, as your brother-in-law suggests, if you hold the key to Lady Jolyon's chamber, you are in danger. Perhaps she thought the murderer might decide to kill you first, in order to get it."

"Thus exploding any suggestion of suicide? No, I think not," smiled Justin. "Well, are we to make ready for bed, do you think? I mean, are we here to just mutually protect each other, or is there an end in view?"

"Mutually protect," laughed Guy. "I can take care of myself."

"Not if you are asleep, you can't," said Justin. "Besides which, you do need protection. Not, I'll agree, from a would-be murderer, but from the charge of murder. Hal has astutely made sure that if anything occurs tonight, Lady Jolyon will have several witnesses to her innocence. It would seem Bess intends that we shall be provided with proof of our innocence, too."

"By God! I never thought of that," cried Guy looking amazed. "I just thought Westwood was all for locking her away, because he disapproves of our being lovers."

"Never make the mistake of underestimating Hal Westwood," said Justin. "He is a very clever fellow, unfortunately, his weak spot is his father's reputation and family honour."

"Yet, I've heard it said, Sir Francis Westwood doesn't give a damn about his honour."

"Quite," said Justin bitterly. "That's why Hal must work twice as hard at it, to paper over the cracks."

Guy laughed at that and took a draught of his wine saying, "Come, tell me more of this venture we were discussing last night, Danvers. Is the ship your father's? Will it trade from Bristol?"

"Yes, from Bristol to Kingston. My father's cousin Eunice, who lives near Chawcester, has a nephew, on her late husband's side of the family, who is a sea captain. He is in partnership with a merchant in Bristol. They need money to cargo the ship. My father is prepared to risk a certain sum, and is talking to interested parties. I gather Hal's father has advanced monies and Hal is thinking of putting some in. Why, are you interested?"

Guy shrugged his shoulders. "I would that I had enough spare cash about me," he replied bluntly.

"It is thought to be a great opportunity," said Justin. "My father looks to vastly increase his fortune for a modest sum. The risk of course, is in the voyage, but the returns are good, if it is successful."

"Yes I'll—"

"Hist! What is that noise?" Justin interrupted him.

"The murderer come for the key," hissed Guy leaping to his feet with great agility, and snatching up his swordbelt. "Don't worry, he'll not get past me."

"Nor me," snapped Justin tartly, not liking the suggestion he needed the protection of another man. "Shush, listen!"

Guy frowned, "It sounds like women squealing."

A tiny squeal confirmed this opinion, and a moment

later came the sound of fingers brushing against wooden panelling. As they both stood transfixed, staring at a place beside the hearth, slowly, with a sound like a low rumble of distant thunder, the panel slid back to reveal a dusty and dishevelled Mary, with Bess standing behind her.

"Mary!" cried Guy. That one word expressed all the love and anxiety he endured. "Oh, Mary, my love." He hurried forward to help her out and clasped her gently in his arms.

"So, madam wife, this was your plan," said Justin grinning, as he helped Bess from the dusty passage, and removed several long cobwebs from her shiny hair.

"Not mine, but Mary's," she replied simply. "I was, but the messenger." She clasped the edges of his coat firmly, holding him fast. "Dear God, Justin, that was not an experience I'd care to repeat." She glanced uneasily over her shoulder to the darkened void behind the panelling.

"I'm afraid we must go back presently, Bess," said Mary. Her face glowed as she tried to disengage from Guy's ardent embrace. "Mr Danvers, I do beg pardon for this intrusion, but quite frankly, the thought of never seeing Guy again with any privacy has made me bold."

"Ma'am, I am honoured to be allowed to repay the

great debt I owe you, in some measure," replied Justin slowly. "I am only amazed my chamber should be so opportune."

"No, I planned it so," she replied taking the seat Guy indicated and cast him another shy, grateful smile, as he retained hold of her hand, kissing it. "I thought if the news of your wedding were to break, and Hal were to be absolutely impossible, you and Bess could meet here unbeknown to any, and even, if necessary, make your escape."

"Why? Does it lead to the outside?" asked Guy, his attention taken.

"Well, yes, so Sir Edward always claimed," she said doubtfully. "Truth to tell, although I knew of its existence, this was the first time I'd ever used it. But the steps do go down beyond my chamber, and are supposed to lead past the orchard, and come out in Grove Wood."

"And is the tunnel passable?" asked Guy eagerly, a plan formulating in his head.

"I don't know," she said frowning. "I seem to recollect Sir Edward saying there had been a cave-in at one point, but I also know he regularly used the passage at one time, much like a privy stair."

"Then what do we wait for, sweetheart?" he replied

impatiently. "Let us gather your cloak and be away from this cursed place."

"Leave?" asked Mary blankly.

"At once," he replied gaily.

"I rather think not, Armstrong," said Justin.

"You think not?" Guy laughed. "I'd like to see you try to stop me."

"Should the necessity arise, I will do so," snapped Justin, nettled by his laughter. "However, a few minutes pause, should give you both time to think for yourselves. Firstly, as I pointed out to that offensive fellow, Soames, there is near two foot of snow out there, a blizzard raging and drifting. I doubt very much you'd even be able to leave the protection of Grove Wood, should your passage lead so far. Secondly, and much more importantly, if Lady Jolyon were innocent, then the very worst thing she could do is to run away. All would instantly believe her guilty. Thirdly, I have given my word none should have the key to her chamber. Granted, I did not then know of this secret passage, but the principle remains the same. As I pointed out to you earlier, Lady Jolyon is indeed safest under lock and key, for as Hal foresaw, none can harm her, and if, as he seems to believe, our murderer is none too bright, her innocence could now be proved beyond doubt."

"I hear what you are saying, Danvers, and there is some truth in it," agreed Guy. "But didn't you take in what was said in the parlour earlier this evening? Sir Edward is dead, poisoned by a punch brewed by his wife. A wife, who freely admits to adding something to the punch, something moreover, given to her by a witch. A wife, who has every reason in the world for wanting to be rid of her husband. None will believe her innocence."

"I do," he replied firmly.

"Yes, we who know and love her, cannot but believe in her. There is no question that she is innocent. But does the same faith apply to the average man? Did you not see that fat constable's face? Once her child was spoken of, he'd tried and condemned her in his own mind. You, of all people, must know of the penalty for a woman found guilty of murdering her husband by witchcraft."

Bess gasped in horror, "No—no, they wouldn't—they don't still—"

"Indeed, they do still burn witches!" insisted Guy. "So come, my pretty, back to your chamber. We need warm boots for your feet and several cloaks."

"But, Guy," cried Mary, who was white to the lips at these revelations, "Where would we go? They would hunt us down like animals, and your house would be their first destination."

"Yes, if we are lucky, they'll waste time going there, but we shall not. Don't worry, sweetheart, I'll see you are safe. I've made my plans; this has only hastened them."

"What plans?" cried Bess, tears gathering in her eyes. "Oh, Mary, what shall we do?"

"Sit down and discuss this like rational creatures," said Justin crisply. "Armstrong, you are in a panic. There is no hard proof Lady Jolyon poisoned her husband. There's not enough evidence to hang a dog on. It's all coincidence. A clever advocate would ensure that was understood by the jury."

"Aye, and it would be totally ignored," he returned swiftly. "There is nothing your average village dullard dislikes more, than a fine lady caught out in sin. I tell you once they know she has a lover, it won't matter her husband was the greatest brute that ever lived. They'll fall over themselves to condemn her. Each and every man on that jury will be married, or thinking of it, and if he doesn't condemn adultery, then who knows where it might break out next. In his own wife, perhaps?"

"No, no," cried Justin impatiently. "You are saying she'll be tried for adultery. That isn't so."

"She'll not only be tried, she'll be found guilty," declared Guy trenchantly. "I know these country juries, and I'm not prepared to run the risk. Mary, don't you trust me, sweetheart? I tell you, I have it all thought out. Indeed, I've thought of little else since you told me of the baby. You see, Fanny is pretty settled now. I've written instructions for her, explaining that we have no choice, but to leave. I've told her she is to sell our home, Knowle Hall, dividing the proceeds between her and Cecily, as their dowries. Initially, I'd meant to take Cecily with us, but now I'll have to leave her in Fanny's care, until we are established. Then, perhaps, she can come to us."

He hesitated, loosening the grasp he'd taken of her icy, cold hands. "The only thing is, my love, do you have any ready cash? I have a few guineas on me, but we need a fair sum to pay for our passage, and other necessities of the journey. I suppose if we are desperate we can sell the horses, but quite frankly I'd sooner have nothing which could be called Sir Edward's."

"Horses, passage," faltered Mary, "but where are we going, Guy?"

"Virginia," he replied promptly. "To the colony in Virginia. I have some acquaintances there, who will take us in. We can't stop, of course. We'll have to move fairly swiftly, but, under assumed names, none will know of us. I'd planned to travel as cousins, you recently widowed; me penniless, on account of the war; Then, we could be married at a later date, but now that doesn't matter. We can be married immediately, in Bristol, before we set sail."

"What? Wait, you go too fast. To Virginia?" cried Mary aghast. "To go and leave everything behind? To leave my home, my family? To go to the other side of the world, and never come back?"

"I very much regret, Lady Jolyon, that should you flee to Virginia, you could never return," said Justin austerely. "You would be assumed guilty and sentenced in your absence, a sentence which would immediately come into force, should you return to England."

"My darling, what have you here that's so precious?" Guy asked, as she looked knocked asunder by all this. "You speak of home and family, yet your home has already passed into the possession of your husband's heir. Only that which you brought with you, may you take away, and that was precious little, as I remember you telling me. As for your family, I'll be your new family. I and my child. Can you really care so much for those here, who are so ready to find you guilty?"

"None of us think Mary guilty!" cried Bess indignantly.

"None, even your brother, Hal?" he countered.

"I have already explained Hal's position to you," said Justin coldly. "He may find it impossible to condone Lady Jolyon's adultery, but I'll stake my life on him defending her innocence of murder. He'll go right up to the King himself. In fact, he went that high before, for his father, when he was falsely accused. Recollect, ma'am, how tireless Hal was in defence of your father. That case looked worse, yet your father is a free man today."

"But not an untarnished one," cried Guy. "I don't know how many times I've heard it said Sir Francis Westwood got away with murder! That he owed his life to his dealings with the King. He wasn't found innocent, he was pardoned."

"Proof was laid before judge and jury of how another man killed Sir Francis's brother. Sir Francis was found not guilty," said Justin firmly. "I know, for it was my own father who defended him, from a case I prepared myself."

"He still had a free pardon to back it up, and so the jury knew," spat Guy.

"Please, please," cried Bess, as both grew angrier. "It doesn't help for us to quarrel. Mary, what do you think you should do for the best?"

Mary, who was shaking with fear, sank to the edge of the bed, grasping the massive carved post for support. "I'd like to flee," she whispered. "Oh, I'd like so to run away with Guy, to escape from all this trouble and turmoil, but I know it would be hopeless. The wassailers couldn't get more than a dozen yards beyond the gatehouse. They found the snow so deep, and the blizzard so thick, they were forced back, and must sleep the night before the kitchen fire. Oh Guy, Guy, I am so afraid. I know I am innocent, yet I fear they'll have no mercy on me at all!"

"Mary, I give you my word. I'll get you away. A parcel of stupid, drunken churls trying to make their way through snowdrifts, is a different matter to us escaping from Grove Wood. The snow will be lighter under the trees, and it's no more than three miles from there to the high road. I'll find a way."

"Aye, and leave tracks for all to follow," said Justin. "That is, if you don't perish of cold in a snowdrift long before daybreak. Lady Jolyon, I tell you truly, if the weather were better, I, too, might advise you to make good your escape. All Armstrong says is true, but in this weather you would surely perish. Understand, it is yet still snowing and blowing hard. I beg you will therefore remain here and, I swear to you, I will put forth my best efforts to find the murderer and prove you innocent."

"And if you fail?" Guy demanded angrily, as Mary looked undecided.

Justin hesitated, "If I fail to find the murderer, and things still look black, then I will personally bring two stout horses to you in Grove Wood, the moment the thaw sets in."

Chapter Fifteen

Ned, on a hard bench at the head of the gallery, was unable to sleep, what with the events of the afternoon, and the intense cold. The soughing of the wind through the trees sounded just like the stealthy movement of someone in the darkness beyond him. His mind knew what the noise was, but in his over excited state he couldn't quite dismiss thoughts of the ghostly lady of Sidworth Castle. Of course, it was the weather outside, but it did have the uncanny sound of a silken gown.

Eventually, he abandoned the idea of getting any sleep. He got from the bench, swathed his cloak about him, and strode back and forth along the gallery, pondering on what had gone before.

Sir Edward's murder was at the forefront of his mind, but that was soon passed over for thoughts of Cecily. For a while, he dwelt lovingly on her sweet face and words.

Finally, he turned, as bidden by Justin earlier, to consider in detail the events immediately preceding the murder. He came to the conclusion, almost at once, that as a witness, he was no use at all having seen very little of the happenings. He'd been more concerned with watching Cecily's expressive face, than watching the mummers.

However, he remembered St George—who had been revealed to be Zac Drew, the blacksmith and constable, —lifting the silver bowl up high and crying "Wassail!" in ringing tones. As he thought of it again, he saw, in his mind's eye, Drew fumbling with the bowl before bracing himself to lift it. Could it be possible Drew added the poison in that second? Drew was, of course, one of the many who had access to the punch, yet, he had barely been questioned, for, once was known he was the constable, his innocence had been accepted.

After a few minutes further reflection, Ned turned from the gallery, going swiftly down to the first floor, where Hal kept vigil. Ned was certain this thought was worth disturbing him for.

In the event Hal did not need waking. True, he was stretched out full length on the settle he'd occupied the night before. He even had a folded blanket under him, but he lay on his back with his arms behind his head.

His eyes were shadowed with wakefulness and, judging from the look about his handsome mouth, his thoughts far from pleasant.

"Hal," said Ned softly, as he came down the last flight of stairs, "Can you not sleep?"

"No," he replied curtly. "Can you not either?"

"Too cold!" said Ned. He went to the nearest of the hearths and kicked the embers of the fire into life before putting another log on it. "Brrrr, that's better, by heaven. 'Tis bitter cold up in that gallery." He glanced over his shoulder at his prone brother, "Armstrong's not come to bed yet, either."

"No? Well, I thought I heard him ask Justin if he might consult him on a legal matter," replied Hal wearily.

"Hal, I've been thinking," said Ned, after a lengthy pause, in which he managed to get warm.

"Have you? So have I," Hal sighed, his voice sounding bitter.

"Yes, well, you remember how Justin said we were to turn the events over in our minds. To see it again in effect?"

Hal, whose exhausted brain had endlessly pictured Libby's cold face quoting the Bible to him, merely nodded grimly.

"Well, I've been thinking and, well, truth to tell, I

only recollect St George raising the bowl on high and crying 'Wassail!'."

"Yes, I observed your thoughts and eyes elsewhere for most of the feast," replied Hal, a glimmer of a smile chasing away the gloom of his countenance. "Have you got it bad? Is it your first time in love?"

Ned met his eyes with dignity. "Yes, it is the first time, the only time."

"One always thinks that," Hal yawned prodigiously.

"No, Hal, this is it," said Ned firmly. "I shall write to Father and speak to her brother."

"Father won't like it," Hal replied bluntly. "They've no money at all, and are like to be plunged into scandal when Armstrong is charged with murder."

"Yes, I saw the resemblance to our family at once," retorted Ned, "and Armstrong is no more guilty of murder than I am. Don't worry, I don't ask for your support. I can fight my own battles with Father."

Hal shrugged and yawned again, moving stiffly into a sitting position, "That must be your decision," he said, in his most discouraging manner.

"I wanted to talk to you about St George, Hal. He's the blacksmith fellow, the constable. Do you recall him lifting that punch bowl on high?" Ned asked.

"Yes, I believe so," replied Hal. "He gave a great cry

as he did, did he not? I remember thinking he was well chosen for the part. It needed someone with great strength to lift that bowl."

"Yes, indeed, but cast your mind back to slightly before. The dragon is slain, and going through death throes before the fire. St George has tried to claim his bride and got a smack in the mouth, for trying to kiss the choir boy." He paused and Hal nodded, frowning as with an effort as he tried to remember all this. "Then St George turned to the bowl set before the fire. Do you recall?"

"No," said Hal, "no, at that moment little Harry asked if the dragon was really dead, and I didn't look up again until St George called 'Wassail', as he raised the bowl."

"Damn!" said Ned, "That was exactly the moment that, it seems to me, he fumbled with something. Fumbled almost in the act of lifting."

"'Tis surely a heavy weight filled with punch, perhaps he was just adjusting his grip?" Hal suggested.

"No, it was something more than that. Or, at least I thought it was," he ended, doubt sounding in his voice.

"What possible reason could the blacksmith have for wanting to kill Sir Edward?" Hal asked reasonably.

"I don't know," replied Ned, "but we've not even

considered it. Don't you see, because he is also the constable, we've assumed he must be innocent."

"True," agreed Hal, "and he did have an unparalleled opportunity. He knew he'd be giving the bowl directly to Sir Edward, and needed only to hesitate, as indeed he did, to be safe."

"Exactly!" cried Ned, satisfied Hal was taking the matter more seriously now.

"Hmm, it does seem to bear investigation," said Hal thoughtfully. "We must discuss it with Justin to see what he thinks and try, if we can, to discover something of the local gossip. Perhaps the fellow has some reasons to hate Sir Edward," he sighed. "Indeed, I shouldn't think it would be difficult to discover quite a few people, who wanted Sir Edward dead. He was, by all reports, a most unpleasant fellow."

"Yes, he was, but unfortunately, none have so great a reason for his death as Mary and Armstrong," said Ned as he moved about restlessly. He was still not completely warm, and rather irked that his brother had laughed at his love for Cecily. He'd been hoping for the opportunity to confide his dreams, but Hal had dismissed them as unimportant. He felt affronted. "I think I'll see if I can discover any gossip now," he said after a pause.

"Now, in the middle of the night?" asked Hal.

He blinked, aware he'd disappointed his prickly brother.

"It's not far off of five of the clock," said Ned. "Some-one should be stirring in the kitchen by now. The kitchen or stables are usually the most reliable source of gossip. Either way, I'd like a mug of mulled ale, wouldn't you?"

"Yes, very much so," Hal agreed and groaned as he eased his back into a more comfortable position, think-ing over a mug of ale with Ned might be able to repair matters.

Ned put another log on the fire and glanced at the locked door Hal was guarding. "Have you heard any-thing from Mary?"

"Not a thing since she stopped weeping, around mid-night," replied Hal. "Hopefully, she cried herself to sleep."

"She's safest there. It was a clever idea of yours, Hal," Ned remarked as he walked off towards the stairs.

Hal propped himself in a corner and closed his eyes, a little heartened by Ned's praise. He dozed fitfully, but he woke immediately he heard a step on the stair.

"Hal?" Libby came tentatively towards him, her fur-lined cloak over her nightgown. "Were you sleeping? I'm sorry. I didn't mean to awaken you."

"I was only dozing," he replied. He sat up again and, making room for her beside him on the settle, said, "It's impossible to sleep properly on this damned, uncomfortable thing."

"Poor, Hal," she said lightly, "need you remain here?"

"Yes, I must. I'm still worried about Mary. She's fool enough to go wandering about these ill-lit passages at night and get herself killed, too." He scanned her face anxiously, "Could you not sleep either?"

"No, I am too cold," she replied, "but I have Harry tucked up fast asleep close to the fire."

"Come, sit by me. I'll warm you," he said and opened his own cloak.

She snuggled down into his arms, glad of the warmth of his body, laying her head on his chest. His arms tightened about her and he kissed the top of her head.

"Are you still very cross with me?" he asked quietly.

"A little," she admitted. "You were so censorious, so implacable."

He sighed. "It looks so bad, Libby," he said, as if by way of an excuse.

"Yes, I agree it does look dreadful, but recriminations don't help. Mary knows, knew, from the beginning, you would never approve her conduct. There is no need to say so, especially in public."

"There is need, Libby, don't you see, if she's not careful her behaviour will hang her," he cried quickly. "If only she had not been such a fool as to add that love-potion, or if she'd not been carrying Armstrong's child. By God, you'd think at the very least she'd have tried to pass it off as Sir Edward's child!"

"That would have involved deceit of the most despicable kind!" Libby was shocked, "If she loves Guy Armstrong, how could she even thinking of lying with her husband."

"She has no business loving Guy Armstrong," he said impatiently then, as she glanced to him again, he nodded adding, "Yes, just the same as I had no business loving my step-mother Jacqueline. Just because I've sinned in the past, it doesn't mean her sin is any the less. Besides, none knew of that beside you and I, and you've forgiven me."

"Your father knew," Libby remarked quietly.

"My father? No, he cannot have done," cried Hal aghast. "Jacqueline would never have confessed."

"He knew all the same," she continued relentlessly. "I saw it in his face. He said he'd take Jacqueline back to France to avoid further trouble."

"Between her and Bess," He insisted sharply.

"No, Hal," she glanced to him again. "I knew what he meant. And he knew, I knew what he meant."

"Nonsense," he cried, much put out. "He cannot have done so. You must be imagining it."

♣

Whilst Hal was coming to terms with this unwelcome knowledge, Ned made his way to the kitchens at the rear of the hall. They were the old-fashioned type of kitchens, build of wood, under a thick thatch, with only the chimney of brick, tacked on to the end wall of the castle hall. The pantry and buttery were empty, but the big main kitchen, with its vast fireplace still warm, was awash with humanity. The mummers were all snoring loudly after the vast quantities of ale they'd consumed. Ned hurried on into the stillroom, which was quieter. He could hear someone moving about.

"Good morrow," he said, pausing in the doorway with the two mugs of ale he'd filled in the buttery. "May I make use of your fire to warm my ale?"

The plump, pleasant-faced, old woman, who sat before the fire engaged in plucking a fine, fat goose, nodded agreeably, and made room for him. "Indeed, you may, and be welcome, young master. Put that sack of feathers to one side, and sit yourself where 'tis warm."

Ned squatted on a stool as bid, thrusting the poker into the heart of the fire. "'Tis a bitter night," he remarked as he cast his eyes to the window. The shutters were creaking as the wind howled about the castle. A faint chink of light suggested dawn was not as far distant as he thought.

"Indeed, 'tis," she agreed.

"Yet you are up betimes," he said hoping to lead her into discussion.

"Aye, well, 'tis best to be up and about the Lord's business early on," she replied comfortably. "Afore other folk gets under foot, so to speak. Give me an hour afore dawn, I always say, and I'll accomplish more on my own, than three in the afternoon, with a dozen wenches, at my beck and call."

Ned nodded, "I've observed it to be so," he agreed. "My sister must find you a great boon."

"Aye, poor lady," the woman sighed, and shook her head sadly.

There was a short pause, as both plainly recollected the previous day's events, then Ned said lightly, "It will not make your tasks any easier this morn, to have those fellows from the village camped about your fire in the kitchen."

"The reason you find me in here, young master," she

replied grimly, plucking so furiously that the down rose about her in a flurry. "I'd not normally do this in here, but there's no getting close to the kitchen fire today."

"I expect you know all those fellows well though, don't you?" remarked Ned as he began rubbing his feet briskly to bring back the warmth in them.

"Aye, well enough," she replied. "Them, and their mothers afore 'em, like as not."

"A good set of men?" he asked.

"Good enough, think on," she replied, glancing shrewdly to him. "Like most folks, there's them who say a mite too much in their cups, and the odd one who's over-handy with his fits, but by-and-large, a decent set of men."

"The blacksmith, now, he who played St George, he's a fine figure of a man," said Ned idly. "I'm thinking he's well fitted for his part of dragon slaying."

"Aye, Zac Drew has played St George since I don't know when," she nodded. "There's his lad, Toby waiting on the part these past five year, but Zac won't have it. He do love to get himself up in all that mummery, he do."

Ned smiled, "Is his lad a blacksmith, too?" he asked.

"Aye, though he ain't the strapping fellow of his sire. No, he were bred a mite finer on his dam's side."

"Has he but the one son?" asked Ned, wondering how he was to ever bring the discussion round to the blacksmith's relationship with the late lord of Sidworth Castle.

"Aye, six daughters and but the one lad, and him the sickly, puny, brat, they never thought to rear. Six strapping lasses, up to every bit of mischief and larks, and one lad who'd fain be a poet."

Ned chuckled, "A poet! I can't see any father being pleased at that, certainly not mine."

The old woman shook her grey locks, joining him in a gap-toothed laugh. "Aye, Zac had no easy time of it when his Betty died giving birth to the lad. Not with Toby, and the youngest lass. For, whilst the boy is as meek as milk and water, his sister is a firebrand, who's a disgrace to the village. Zac will have his work cut out getting her safely wed, like her sisters, and no mistake."

"Like as not she'd get wed herself," murmured Ned thinking of Bess. He realised with a start of surprise it was only twenty-four hours since her wedding.

"Happen that it's already too late," agreed the woman darkly. She looked about and leaned forward over her goose. "I've seen her slipping out of the castle at first light often," she hissed. "Meg is so up in the boughs about being Sir Edward's leman, but she weren't the only one, not by a long chalk she weren't. Past counting they'd be, the women the master took to his bed."

"I'll be bound," said Ned pricking up his ears. "And the constable's daughter one of them?"

"Aye, Clary, the youngest. A big, strapping wench she be. Eyesome like, and full of sauce, that's the type the master liked best. She'd been coming here all through last summer and autumn, night after night."

"Was Zac Drew pleased at this? Did he think he might find advancement with Sir Edward?" asked Ned doubtfully.

"No, not he," cried the woman. She picked up the goose, holding it close to the flames to singe off the last of the feathers, and tossed it to the table, before picking up another from a pile at her feet, and beginning all over again. "No, Zac Drew, he had some book learning with the old parson, you see. What with that, and him being a solider in the war, he got some odd notions into his head. Aye, proper gone moonstruck, we reckoned, when he came back from the fighting. Chock full of them ideas, about all men being made equal. Aye, now, what were it he used to chant? Aye that's it, 'When Adam delved and Eve span, who were then the gentlemen?' Daft we called 'e and that made him quite wild. Used to curse us, he did, as fools unborn. Aye, but he's been quiet these last few years, since the King has got his own again."

"Not the sort of man to take the seduction of his daughter in good part?" Ned suggested tentatively.

"Seduction? I don't reckon that'd be no seduction," grinned the old woman. "She'd be more than willing, would Clary! A draggletail, if ever I saw one. Not that it would make any difference, as far as Zac were concerned. Mercy upon us! What ails the lad?"

She broke off clutching the goose to her, as the door to the courtyard was thrust open, letting in a blast of bitter air. A lad, skinny and blue-faced with cold, tumbled into the stillroom, his eyes wild, and his lips trembling.

"She's—she's dead!" he gasped, flinging out an arm, which visibly shook. "Out there in the snow. Dead. Blood everywhere—dead!"

"Dead? Who is dead?" cried Ned as he leapt to his feet. Hal's fears of the previous night were still uppermost in his mind, whilst the lad leaned against the doorjamb, as if his legs would no longer hold him.

"Meg," said the boy, ashen lipped. "Dead, out there—butchered on the midden!"

"Good God," cried Ned, "quickly, lad, show me."

He hastened after the boy into the unearthly white light, and hush that comes after night of snow. He could see by the single row of steps, how the lad had left the stable to ease himself, and stopped dead at the sight of Meg. The maid was lying akimbo on the whitened mound of the dung heap.

♣

Ned was well used to the sight of blood. He'd seen beasts ridden down in the chase, and torn apart at his very feet, but this, this was different. Whether it was because she was another human being, or because of the stark contrast of the blood on the snow, he felt the gorge rise in his throat, and had to look away hastily.

His brain was racing as he turned abruptly, hurried into the stillroom, and on into the kitchen. He was intent on seeing if the blacksmith were absent from the sleeping group about the fire.

Zac Drew was, however, part of the group gathered about the cook. All were talking excitedly and waving their arms. The opportunity had been missed. If only he could have found Zac Drew gone, or still sleeping soundly, that matter could have been settled but, no, it wasn't to be that easily solved. Ned recollected his ale and turned back for it, pushing aside the excited throng, as they clustered in the doorway, exclaiming over the body of the wench.

A sudden thought occurred to Ned, and he followed them to the door, as a few hardier souls approached the body. "Drew," he called sharply. "Allow none to touch the corpse."

All turned their faces to him, registering either surprise or amazement. "We wouldn't do that," said one slowly. "'Tis death to disturb a murdered soul. They do walk!"

Ned raised his brows in surprise and turned back into the castle wondering how Cecily would take this news of another ghost that walked. He hurried upstairs to find Hal and Libby both asleep on the hard settle, with Hal's arms firmly clasped about her. Ned paused for a moment, a faint smile curving his lips at the sight, thinking how he's like to sleep thus with Cecily. Then with a sigh, he bent to shake Hal awake. "Hal," he murmured quietly. "Hal, wake up."

Hal opened his eyes slowly, looking as if he were drugged with sleep. "Ned?" he muttered, then as Libby moved in his arms, he awoke more fully. "Ned, what is it?"

"Meg, Mary's wench—she's dead!" he replied succinctly.

"Meg?" Hal sat up abruptly, clasping the sleepy Libby to his chest, and glanced wildly about the gallery.

"Mary? Where is she?"

"She is still abed, 'tis barely dawn," soothed Ned. "See your plan worked. Mary is cleared."

"What plan?" Libby was still fogged with sleep. "Where is Mary?"

"Ned, knock on the door, if you will," commanded Hal. "I would like to hear Mary's voice and be sure all is well."

"Here, take this then," said Ned and he handed him the mug of ale. Hal took it and sipped, handing it on to Libby, who was shivering. "Drink up, Libby, it's hot."

"Mary!" Ned raised his voice a little, and knocked imperatively on the worn oak door, "Mary, 'tis I, Ned. Are you there?"

Hal got to his feet and came to join him, "Mary! Mary! Come to the door."

There were some muffled sounds from within, and then Mary's voice, sounding frightened, came through the stout panels. "Ned, Hal, what's the matter?"

"Oh, thank God," said Hal simply, "thank God. Listen Mary, your woman, Meg, she's been murdered."

"Meg, dead?" Mary's voice rose, sounding amazed, disturbed, and then tearful.

"Yes, and don't fret, for it as good as clears you of Sir Edward's murder," said Hal. "Listen, I want you to open the door."

"I can't, Hal," she replied. "You locked me in."

"So I did," he cried shaking his head. "I am still half-mazed with sleep. Ned, run and fetch Justin, if you please. He has the key."

♣

Ned set off for Justin's chamber and in a few moments returned with Justin and Guy Armstrong.

"Is it so?" Justin asked as he handed the key to Hal. "Has Lady Jolyon's maid been found dead?"

"So Ned says," replied Hal, unlocking the door. "That clears Mary, does it not?"

"On the face of it, it seems unlikely we'd have two murderers," agreed Justin. "How was she killed Ned?"

"Her throat was cut," said Ned starkly. "Out on the midden."

"Outside?" frowned Hal, as the door swung open.

"Yes," Ned answered shortly. He was still upset by the thought of the body.

"But how odd," said Justin, "Why should the wench go out on such a wild night?"

"To answer a call of nature?" Guy Armstrong said frowning over the suggestion, as Bess and Mary, both looking frightened, huddled in the doorway.

"Not in a snowstorm, surely?" asked Libby.

"Wait," said Justin, "The snow. Was the body covered in snow, Ned?"

"No, blood," replied Ned.

"How horrid!" cried Mary, as tears filled her eyes again, "Poor Meg!"

"Not covered in snow, yet bled a lot," Hal said thoughtfully.

"Dead sometime then?" asked Justin, meeting his eyes. "Well, this alters things considerably. I'm going to take a look at her. Do you come, Hal?"

Hal nodded, "Yes, I suppose we'd better." His eyes travelled from Libby to Mary, being consoled by Bess. "I think you should all remain here— and together."

"I must go to little Harry and Alys," cried Libby. "I hadn't truly realised the danger we stand in. Why, any may be attacked!"

"No," Hal caught her hands, his voice soothing. "Be calm, my dear, do not panic. None shall harm you, or little Harry. You've seen nothing, and know nothing. It is a different matter for Mary." He turned to include them all. "Understand me! Mary must never be left alone at any time, for she, if possible, is now in even greater danger. It will soon become plain she is innocent, and now the murderer is desperate."

Mary clutched Guy's arm, her face white. "Oh, who can it be?" she whispered, "Who can it be?"

"Well, we now know it's not you, or Bess," said Justin. "And Mr Armstrong and I can swear as to where we were last night. Whilst Hal was here on this settle, as no doubt his aching bones will verify."

"That only leaves you and I, Libby, with no clear proof," grinned Ned. "Although I've a witness since I left you, Hal, for I've been sitting before the kitchen fire with the cook."

"And Libby was with me," said Hal. "Come, this is excellent progress. At least we can be sure of each other. Your sisters, Armstrong, do they not share a bed? Not that I am seriously considering them, you understand, but 'tis better if we can eliminate all we can."

"Yes, they do, and Fanny swears she seldom sleeps the night through, so no doubt the slightest sound would disturb her. Does that mean they are clear of suspicion?"

"Indeed," nodded Justin, "that leaves Sir Walter, his wife and son, and the men from the village."

"The blacksmith had a good reason to wish Sir Edward ill," said Ned remembering the cook's tale.

"Does he?" Hal's interest was stirred. "Yes, we must

all meet to discuss matters in say, half an hour—after Justin and I have seen the body? Mary—all of you— please keep together! And someone waken the Mistresses Armstrong, then keep them with you also."

Chapter Sixteen

Dismissed, Ned sped away on the errand, which appealed to him. Guy assured himself everyone was safely in Mary's chamber and then went with Hal and Justin to see the body.

"Cecily!" cried Ned as he entered the gallery and saw Cecily standing looking out the window at the snow. "Didn't a servant call to you, to tell you not to be alone at any time?"

"Yes," she replied with a smile, "but Fanny is in the chamber, and I knew you'd come as soon as you could."

"Do you understand? Did Mary's servant not make it clear?" Quickly he came to her side. "You know her woman Meg has been killed?" He took her hand, which trembled slightly. "Are you not afraid to stand here alone?"

"I am not alone," she replied, smiling at his fears. "Fanny is by, and now you are come. Ned, I've something I want to tell you."

"Have you? What is it?" He returned the pressure of her hand gently.

"Well, firstly, I love you," she replied with a smile.

"Oh Cecily," he murmured his thoughts instantly diverted, "you are an angel." He gazed at her a few seconds with longing, and then recollected himself. "No, come, we mustn't be tempted down fancy's by-ways. What is it you must tell me?"

"It—it's about something—something I overheard yesterday," she confided, as he drew her into a window seat and they sat down. "Do you recollect Mr Danvers said last night to think over what had happened very carefully? Well, I did, and I remembered something, only—only—I don't like to go to Mr Danvers. He is so serious and preoccupied—and I'd feel so very silly if it was nothing."

"It wouldn't matter," he replied, "but anyway, tell me and I'll pass on the message. Remember he said it didn't matter how insignificant it was."

"Yes, but this is so unimportant, at least it seemed so to me at the time," she replied wrinkling her smooth forehead, in a manner he found enchanting. "It was yesterday, you know, before it all happened, before Sir Edward was poisoned, when I was helping Lady Jolyon."

"Yes, I remember you were doing that," he agreed, wondering what was coming next.

"The men from the village, the mummers, arrived to prepare for the play, but they were early and so Lady Jolyon bade me show them into that small chamber. You know, the one next to the parlour, so they might get into their mumming clothes."

"Yes," he nodded his understanding.

"I showed them the way, and saw that they had candles, for even then it was dark in the chamber. Then I returned to my task, I was roasting the apples and at that moment Meg called to your sister to attend to something, and I was left alone in the hall. Then, I realised I'd not shut the door to the small chamber properly. I could hear the men laughing, as they got into their costumes—you know how they do—chaffing each other and poking fun and such? Then one of them—I don't know which—said something to the constable— Zac Drew, I think they called him."

"Aye, that's him, the blacksmith," Ned nodded, alert now.

"Oh, I thought he was the constable," she said, looking confused. "Oh well, yes, him. They were all laughing by this time, and then one man said something about Clary."

"His daughter?" he agreed swiftly.

"Well, I gathered she was, for he grew very angry and shouted at them all, saying his Clary were a good girl, and he'd thank them all to remember it. Well, they were dreadfully rude, Ned. At least, I didn't truly understand one half of the things they were saying," she added, her reddening cheeks belying her words. "But then he grew more angry still and shouted—well—he said—well—I can't exactly remember his words, but something like—Sir Edward would need to look out for himself."

"Yes? Truly? Good!" Ned grasped her hands eagerly. "Now listen, this could be vitally important. Try to remember exactly what was said."

Cecily knit her brows and looked like a cross kitten, "Don't you see, that's the trouble. I can't exactly remember? I didn't understand, and that's why I don't want to tell Mr Danvers. He'll say I must remember, and stand over me asking questions, and then I'll get confused, and say something silly."

"No, no, calm down," soothed Ned, seeing she was getting very upset. "Come, snuggle up to me and we'll talk of something else." He turned to look down into the bleak courtyard below, noticing the snow piled high against the walls. "Did you sleep well?"

She smiled up at him, hovering on the verge of tears. "No, no, I did not. My nerves were all on edge, and, of course, poor Fanny has caught a head-cold, so she snored." She made a comical face. "In fact, I got up about midnight, and came out here to see if you, or anybody else, were about and wakeful," she sighed, "but none were, of course."

"Dear God, Cecily!" he cried in horror. "Didn't you truly comprehend the danger?" He held her against him more firmly. "Thank God none were about, especially the murderer. You must promise me, you'll never take such a risk again. You and your sister, indeed, none of the females, must be alone at anytime, until this madman is caught. Now, promise me."

"I promise," she replied docilely. "Although I assure you I was perfectly safe. I often get up and walk about in the night at home, if I can't sleep. It doesn't harm me. In the winter, I either sit before the fire, or watch the moon, as I did last night."

"Watch the moon?" He repeated the words with a quizzical smile. "There was no moon last night, Cecily. It was blowing a blizzard, snow falling so thick, one couldn't see a hand in front of one's face."

"Not all night it wasn't," she replied with a small smile. "It stopped snowing hard not long after midnight, when I first awoke. By the time I came to sit here, about half past the hour, the moon was up, the sky clearing and I was able to see across the courtyard below. It was clear enough to see Mr Soames as he walked to the stables."

"So, Geoffrey Soames was up and about was he?" Ned murmured to himself as, his eyes followed the direction of her finger to the entrance to the stable yard. "You saw him enter the stable yard, you say?" Then as she agreed, he nodded. He knew the dung heap wasn't visible from where they stood. "Now, I wonder what took him there?"

"I don't know, I thought he'd gone to look at his horse. Didn't he say at supper the other night it had a strained hock?"

"Yes," he agreed. "Although, I can't think Soames is a man to care enough for his beasts to go to them on a night like last night. But come, it seems your sister is ready to be escorted to the other ladies, and I must see Hal and Justin, and tell them all you've told me."

It was a matter of moments only to escort both young ladies to Mary's chamber, now bright with a fresh, burning fire and mulled mead.

This done, he took himself off, back down through the deserted Great Hall, which was now free of ghosts in the sharp, clear light of snow. The body of Sir Edward was still laid out on the table, covered only by a cloth. From there, he went into the kitchens, where the servants were huddled in frightened groups, and very little work was being done. He found his companions still at the dung heap. They now had Geoffrey Soames in company with them.

"Because it is clear she was killed after the last fall of snow, yet before the frost," Justin was saying patiently as Ned joined the group. He was relieved to see that a sheet had been laid across the body, too, so that her staring eyes could no longer haunt him. But her blood still stained the whiteness of the snow, and now their footstep were churning it up, making everything appear more ugly than before.

"You'll have observed," Justin continued, lifting the sheet and plainly addressing Geoffrey Soames, who, Ned suspected, had entered some sort of caveat. "that there is little or no snow actually upon her body and that she bled freely. Bled until, one assumes, the frost was so severe as to stop the blood. If only we knew when the snow stopped, we might be able to hazard a time of death."

"Why, Mr Soames must be able to assist us there," said Ned, as he hastened to join in the conversation.

"I?" Soames turned quickly, seeing him for the first time. "Why should I be able to help you?"

"According to Mistress Cecily Armstrong, who suffered a wakeful night after the tribulations of the day, she saw you cross to the stable yard at about half an hour after midnight. She further says, the blizzard stopped at midnight, and at the time she saw you, there was enough moon to see you quite clearly."

All present turned to stare at Geoffrey Soames, who looked confounded by these revelations.

"What were you doing out on such a wild night?" Hal asked bluntly, voicing the question on all their minds.

"I—I needed some air," he replied, ill at ease, but taking a lofty tone. "I assume a man may take the air, if he wishes?"

"Indeed," agreed Hal, "but I find it unlikely, given the circumstances of the weather, and the unsettling state of affairs."

"No doubt you do," he snarled, "but then, we're not all tucked up snug with a wife."

"Where exactly did you take your air, Mr Soames?" Justin put the question politely. "Mayhap, you saw something—someone? It cannot have been far from the time, this poor wench was slaughtered."

"Did I not see you talking to Meg earlier? Just before we all retired?" asked Guy Armstrong sharply, as unconsciously the others formed a circle about the cousin of the murdered man.

"Did you?" Soames replied in a blustering tone. "I'd have thought you too hot to bed your leman." He glanced about him warily, as if he felt trapped by their questions.

Justin silenced the retort on Guy's lips with a look. "Were you talking with this poor girl earlier?" He was still polite, but with a quiet air of authority.

"I—I may have exchanged a few words with her, amongst others," Soames replied. Again all eyes were fixed upon his face.

"Why?" Justin asked the question bluntly.

"I cannot see what business that is of yours," Soames snapped in reply.

"Then, you are wrong," said Hal with authority. "For this is murder, Soames. Double murder, most like. And when it's murder, everything becomes everyone's business. None here forget how you gain by Sir Edward's death. Poor Meg, fool that she was, claimed to know the murderer. That is a double motive to silence her. I demand to know why you spoke to her, and what was said."

"Damn you and damn your demands!" Soames, driven into a corner by their questions, turned on them like a cornered rat. "You hold no jurisdiction here."

"Once again, you are wrong," replied Hal calmly. "Every man has a right to demand the truth of another, in a matter of murder. You can refuse to answer, but your refusal shall be noted by us all, and the obvious conclusions reached."

"Damn you! I went to tell her she'd not be thrown out in the cold, now my uncle is dead," he snapped. "To—to offer her my protection, if she required it." He glared at the group of men staring at him with sceptical eyes.

"You must forgive us," said Hal ironically. "We had little idea you'd exhibit such delicacy of thought, to one in distress. I trust she was suitably grateful."

"Did you arrange to meet her?" demanded Justin, as Soames glared at Hal.

"Yes," he agreed, goaded. "Yes, I did then, but she didn't come. She left me standing waiting, the jade. An hour or more I waited, in that cold stable, all for nought."

"But not of malice, poor wench," said Hal gently. "No doubt she would have come, if she could."

"You did not think to look for her?" asked Justin.

"No," he replied arrogantly. "Damn you, it was cold. I am not accustomed to seeking my drabs. They come to me. I was not going out into that weather looking for a whore!"

"Where did you arrange to meet?" Justin said, making no further comment on this explanation, though Guy snorted in disbelief.

"In the stables, as I told you," he replied curtly. "The beasts mean 'tis warmer in there, and one is not likely to be disturbed, once the grooms have bedded down for the night."

"Meg died not twenty yards from you in the stables, yet you heard nothing?" asked Justin frowning.

"No, I sat on a bale of straw. I had a bottle of wine. I just waited, but then, I wasn't listening for anything." He glanced from one hostile face to another. "Why do you all look at me so? She was a whore. Why should I go looking for her? She was to come to me. Only I tell you, I never saw her!"

"Not even on leaving the stable?" asked Hal, frowning.

"No," he replied. "Why should I? One does not gaze upon a dung heap for amusement. Besides, I was chilled to the bone, and in no pretty temper at being made a fool of. I went to seek warmth by the fire and solace in another wine cup. I tell you I had nothing to do with her death."

"If you tell us so, Mr Soames, then, naturally we must take your word for it. Although you must understand, that others in higher authority may demand proof that you didn't meet her," said Justin judicially. "However, I doubt we can do any more good out here. We must ask questions, once again, of the servants." His gaze travelled to the lowering sky. "I am given to understand that the snow is frozen hard all about, and that try as they may, the men from the village have made precious little headway in clearing a path. I am also informed that further falls of snow are likely." He paused stifling a sigh. "I'm afraid we must face the fact that, should this prove so, we shall be forced to spend another, perhaps several, further nights here all together."

"In which case, we must devise better protection for us all," said Hal firmly, "but such matters are better discussed out of this bitter wind. Soames, will you speak to your father? This woman should be removed from the dung heap, and laid out with respect. Placed in the chapel, perhaps? Could you instruct your servants to attend to it?"

On Geoffrey Soames reluctant assent, the group dispersed. Ned hastily followed Hal, and clasped his sleeve murmuring, "I must talk to you, Hal, at once. I've found out something about Zac Drew, and it could be important."

"Have you?" Hal's brow lightened. "Come then, we will discuss it, but first I must see that Libby and little Harry, indeed all the womenfolk, are safe."

Chapter Seventeen

Breakfast was a long, drawn-out meal. Few ate anything, but none seemed inclined to hasten away from the other's company. It was almost as if anyone feared to be alone. Yet none, save perhaps Ned and Cecily, could rest in company, either. The middle hours of the morning frittered away. It was, in fact, much later in the short winter's day that they all met up again, as they gathered at the gate-legged table in the parlour. They were cramped, but preferred it to the huge hall table. Sir Edward's body was now laid out on a bier in the chapel, with the body of his mistress at his feet. Once more, few ate anything of the food, even less was said, and still the snow fell. Finally, the females of the party withdrew to sit by the fire; it seemed the only solace in the bitter land.

"Are you ill, Mary?" Libby asked in an undertone. She drew close to her on a settle, and viewed her pale cheeks with concern.

"No," Mary's smile was brief, and a travesty of its former loveliness. "No, not ill. Hal seems to think it unlikely I'll now be accused of Sir Edward's death. Naturally, I will still have to answer questions, but it looks a lot less black for me, than it did this time yesterday." She sighed and then added half guiltily, "Although, I never wished to gain even this little peace of mind, at the cost of poor Meg's life."

"No, poor soul," agreed Libby as she shuddered. "What an awful way to die. And so cruel, so very wicked to cast her on the dung heap, as if she were nothing."

"Mayhap, Mistress, she is perceived as such by the Lord," interrupted Lady Soames, her snake-like eyes darting maliciously to Mary's face. "He saw her for what she was, an infamous sinner, steeped in lust. Such pain, such death and degradation awaits all fornicators and adulterers."

"Good heavens, my lady, you sound like a Papist," said Libby sharply. "Pain? Death? Sin? What have these to do with us? The good Lord is a forgiving God. If any sin is honestly repented, then He is glad to welcome the sinner back into the arms of His church. No pain or death awaits any that love the Lord."

"Pain and death come to us all, Mistress Westwood," Lady Soames snapped insistently, her eyes flashing. It was almost as if she didn't relish being challenged.

"Indeed, as do joy and mercy, in equal measures," returned Libby. "With each great change in life, comes pain and suffering, and often from them joy and happiness. Certainly, in childbirth, one must suffer to achieve joy. Have you not gained by your kinsman's demise? Has your husband not attained that, which he has waited all his life for, at the expense of another's pain and death?"

The woman threw her a glare of dislike. "Sir Edward was an evil man!" she hissed. "He deserved to suffer pain and death! All who flout the Lord—" She stopped speaking abruptly as her husband entered.

"It would seem Mr Danvers has called his conclave in the hall," Sir Walter said, addressing all the ladies, but fixing an anxious, doubtful look at his wife's face. "He feels it will be easier if we all gather there, now that the body of my cousin and the serving wench are laid out in the chapel. Plainly, we cannot consider a funeral until the weather breaks, and indeed, the rector can return to hold the service." He directed a bow towards Fanny Armstrong, who, for once, was without her embroidery. Even her placidity was finally shaken by the events.

They all rose gladly. The atmosphere of the chamber

had grown unpleasant. It seemed filled with the older woman's venom. Hastily they went out into the Great Hall, where chairs had been drawn up for them beside the huge fire, and the men from the village, and the servants were already assembled.

Justin, taking a seat at a small table, glanced to the group gathered before him. He noted the manner in which the tensions had taken their toll of them all. Few dared to meet another's eyes, and they'd split into family groups, as if seeking shelter and support from their kin.

"Is your sister still laid low by her headache, Mistress Armstrong?" asked Justin with some concern, as he reckoned up their number and found one missing.

"I very much fear so," she replied quietly. "It is always so when Cecily gets over excited. Ned Westwood has been filling her head with nonsense, and now she is quite sickly, so she is laid upon her bed, with a vinegar cloth on her brow."

Justin smiled at Ned's indignant look, "'Tis no great matter. Ned has told me of her observations, and she made a disposition to that effect earlier." He cleared his throat. "This, in itself, is a strictly informal session," he said to the company at large. "It is the same as yesterday, merely a discussion of known facts. So please, any of you, do not hesitate to add anything to the proceedings." He paused for a few seconds and then continued, "I think we must all be aware by now that Lady Jolyon's maid, Meg, was murdered in the course of last night." He paused again, his eyes moving from face to face. Some were pale, and some were grim, only that of Lady Soames was untroubled. "A foul, wicked crime, for she, poor woman, can have known nothing of Sir Edward's murderer. Indeed, it would appear more a desire for attention, than any true knowledge, hastened her end."

"She was ever a heedless, foolish wench," said Mary. Tears filled her eyes suddenly, as she had a fleeting vision of the girl, laughing with another maid only a few days previously. "For all that, she had a good, loving heart, poor thing, and didn't deserve this end."

"A loving heart, especially for your husband, eh, cousin?" sneered Geoffrey. "I'd have thought you, most of all, had cause to hate her, and rejoice in her end."

"I could never rejoice in any violent end," replied Mary quietly. "Poor, foolish girl that she was, she did me no harm, and herself no good, by her ambition."

"No harm! Her end did you much good," he rejoined. "For not only is the slight done to you repaid by her death, but her mouth is effectively stopped. We now have no way of establishing who indeed, did murder your husband."

"I believe we had little likelihood, when she was still alive," said Hal dryly. "Excuse me, but as a justice of the peace I am accustomed to listening to witnesses. Those with something to say, say it. They don't hint, or hold out vague promises; they tell what they know at once. However, on the bonus side of things, by your good offices, Soames, my sister is entirely cleared. For, by your insistence, she was locked the entire night in her bedchamber with my sister for company, and Mr Danvers, again at your instance, held the key."

Justin experienced a qualm at this, and took great care not to meet Bess's eyes. Of course, it wasn't strictly true that Mary hadn't been able to escape from her chamber, but as he had indeed held the key, and she hadn't to his certain knowledge, spent the night alone, he ignored his conscience.

"Exactly," said Justin. "The fact that another murder has taken place makes it extremely unlikely Lady Jolyon was responsible for Sir Edward's untimely end. It is very unlikely there would be two murderers in one gathering. As for this poor maid servant, only a person who thought it likely she had some information, would have found it necessary to murder her."

"It has also been established, by various methods,

that none of us spent the night alone," said Hal. He glanced to Geoffrey Soames, a challenge in his eyes as Justin paused, allowing time for this to sink in. "As I've already said, both my sisters were together. They were locked in my sister Mary's chamber by Mr Danvers, and he sat up in his chamber with Mr Armstrong most of the night, drinking and talking. Armstrong's sisters were also together. My wife was with her child and his nurse, and my brother and I were in consultation. If we can but establish the whereabouts of everyone else, when Meg was killed, I think we could get a long way to establishing the murderer of both Meg and Sir Edward."

"Yes," Justin firmly took control again. "Constable Drew, you were in the company with the men from the village, I believe. Did any of them move all night?"

"Well now, I reckon not, your honour," he replied. He scratched his head, and when he continued it was with some deliberation, "No, not once we'd all settled down, like. There were plenty of tooings and froings earlier on, at say, ten of the clock, or thereabouts, but not after."

"Aye, not after young Jack brought up his boots," cried Tom Greene, the ale draper. There was a burst of unruly laughter at this, from the men of the village.

They were ranged to one side of the hall by the huge oak door, and the young lad in question, who'd played the Egyptian Princess, and who'd been looking remarkably pale, blushed a violent red.

"Brought up his—oh, I see," Justin grinned in sympathy. "Tell me, Jack—which of you is Jack? Ah yes— Jack, did you visit the midden for this exercise?"

"Aye, and Zac guided his steps," said the ale draper, before the lad could speak. "Treated him tender as a wench he did, but then he's had plenty of practice with that lad o' his."

" 'Taint nothing amiss with my lad," said Zac Drew defensively. "He don't go muddling his wits with strong ale."

"No, they're already addled with poesy," cried another of the men, chuckling. "Drunk on words he be! Drunk on words."

"I understand Constable Drew's son is something of a poet," said Hal, as Justin looked amazed, and the constable furious.

"I don't know about that, your honour," he muttered. "He do have his head chock full of dentical-fool notions the rector do encourage, which I'm sure be very kind o' him," he added reluctantly, nodding in Fanny Armstrong's direction.

"What the devil does this have to do with my cousin's

death?" demanded Soames impatiently.

"As like or not, nothing," said Hal calmly, "but gossip has it, that Constable Drew's daughter Clary was a regular visitor to Sir Edward's bed, and we wished to establish whether or not Constable Drew visited the midden last night."

"'Tis a damned lie!" cried the Constable, red-faced with anger. "My Clary weren't nothing to the squire. Came to visit old Alison the cook, she did."

"If you believe that Zac, you're a bigger fool than we did take 'ee for," said the ale draper, glancing to his companions, who nodded. "Why, 'tis well known both Meg and Clary 'ave served Sir Edward this last twelve month."

"'Tis a lie, I tell you!" cried the Constable wrathfully, bringing down his massive fist on the table near him. "My Clary is a good girl!"

"Aye, and I'm the Queen o' Sheba," cried another of the villagers, and they all began laughing again.

"I rather think," said Justin sharply, as the Constable turned on his fellows with furious oaths. "That this is nothing to the purpose. Other than it does establish, Constable Drew, a reason for you wanting to kill Sir Edward."

"Me?" The constable turned back to him, his ruddy

colour fading abruptly, "I didn't 'ave no cause to kill Sir Edward."

"What is more," said Justin, carefully watching him, "you would have had ample opportunity to add poison to the punch, when you presented it to him.

"Nay, nay!" he cried in horror. "I tell 'ee I wouldn't do that! True, I were angered at Squire for taking my Clary's good name, but kill him? Never!"

"Can we speak, young master?" asked Tom Greene getting hastily to his feet, all traces of amusement gone from his weather-beaten face. His companions alongside him on the benches looked concerned, as they saw the sudden turn of events.

"Indeed," said Justin, "any may speak here."

"Zac here, he ain't no poisoner," he said flatly. "He'd knock a man down, aye, like as not, though never to harm him permanent. For he be blacksmith, and he well knows the strength in his arm. Aye, and 'tis true, he's threatened Squire in his rages about Clary, but t'were words, do you see? Kill a man to protect Clary's name? No, that were foolish. Why, if it were so, half the village lads would be corpses by now."

"I see," said Justin dryly, as Hal hid a smile. "Well, as we've discussed at some length, nothing can be proved with regard to Sir Edward's death, but Meg's is different. Can any of you swear an oath, that to your certain knowledge Zac Drew didn't leave the kitchen alone last night?"

"He went to the midden with Jack," said one man, looking confused.

"Alone, you dolt," snapped Tom Greene. "Yes, young master, we don't reckon as he did leave the kitchen fire, but for the time he helped young Jack." He added as the men nodded, "He slept alongside o' you, didn't he, Wat Ferrin?"

"Aye," agreed another younger man, half getting to his feet.

"Did he move all night?" asked Justin again.

"No, if it please your honour," said the man awkwardly, "and I were wakeful, on account of his snoring."

"We all of us slept pretty heavy, what with the ale," said Tom Greene, as another burst of laughter was quickly hushed. He hesitated and then said thoughtfully, "We noticed the dogs were uneasy all night long. They growled as soon as any of us moved, and one barked when you went to the privy, didn't it, Jem?"

"Aye." Another man blushed, and rose to his feet hesitantly. "We put it down to they being the Master's dogs, and knowing as beasts do, when a man is took, so we didn't pay no heed to 'em."

"What time was this?" Justin asked of Jem.

"I, I don't rightly recollect, your honour," he replied, blushing all the more, as all eyes turned on him.

"Was it still snowing? Did you pass the midden? Did you notice ought amiss?" Justin put the questions wearily, as the man became more and more nervous and scratched his balding head. "It were still snowing, but not so furious like, and cold. So cold, as to freeze the marrow of your bones. I didn't linger, if you'll understand me, but one dog, Nimrod, the master's favourite, was sniffing around. He went over to the midden, only I couldn't see why, for on account of the candle in the lantern being low, and it being so cold, so I called to him, and he came back."

Justin nodded in resignation. "And you heard nothing?"

"Well, no," said the man looking embarrassed, "no, not truly hear anything. Only—only the footsteps."

"Footsteps?" repeated Justin, frowning at the fellow.

"The yard, 'tis haunted, your honour," Zac Drew explained, his face pale with fear. "'Tis the Lady of Sidworth Castle, she that did perish in past times. Her ghost do walk."

"Did you see the apparition, the ghost?" asked Justin.

"No, your honour," cried the man, wild-eyed now.

"I ran back to the kitchen as fast as my legs could carry me, and Nimrod followed me. 'Tis certain death to see the Lady of Sidworth Castle. She do hate all men, after what her lord did to her. We all know that. None of us would stay to see the Lady of Sidworth Castle."

"Yes, yes, thank you, we know the legend," said Justin with another sigh. "So in effect, you heard steps, and hastened back to the house?"

"Aye, sir," he replied promptly.

"And Zac Drew, he was there in the kitchen on your return?" he added.

"Sleeping like a baby," grinned the man.

"Then I think we can assume Constable Drew innocent for the moment. However, you may all be required to give evidence at the inquest, at a later date."

"Indeed, your honour," replied the Constable looking relieved, but still shaken. "Thank you, your honour."

"So, if the men of the village are cleared, we can dispense with their presence at once. The same applies to the servants, doesn't it, Lady Jolyon?" suggested Justin.

"Yes," said Mary. "Jackson, who is my—was Sir Edward's steward, examined all the servants earlier. They sleep in the attics. He can vouch for them, you see, and he has charge of them. He says that the only one absent last night was Meg herself. Which wasn't unusual, so none gave a thought to it."

"That leaves only ourselves then," said Justin, as Mary nodded for the servants to go, and they reluctantly filed from the hall. "Ah, Constable Drew, you might remain on duty, if you please. Yes, take a seat there by the door, thank you."

Chapter Eighteen

"Now, to return to matters," said Justin, as the villagers all filed out in the wake of the servants. "You'll remember, indeed I am sure the events of yesterday are still with you, that we parted last night in some disarray. I went with Hal Westwood to lock his sisters in Lady Jolyon's chamber, and thereafter kept the key about my person.

"Whilst still in discussion with Hal Westwood, I was joined by Guy Armstrong, who had seen his own sisters to their chamber. He then accompanied me to my chamber, to consult me on a legal matter. It was a tedious problem, and we drank a good amount of wine in the discussion, with the result Guy fell into a dead sleep before the fire, and I couldn't rouse him. I retired myself, locking my own door and keeping both keys beneath my pillow. I only unlocked the door when Ned Westwood came this morning with news of the girl's death."

"Why did you lock your door?" demanded Geoffrey Soames suspiciously.

"Hal pointed out that he'd unwittingly placed me in some danger. By removing his sister from the murderer's path, he placed me there instead. So I took the simple precaution of locking my door," replied Justin evenly.

"I don't understand all this locking of doors," Sir Walter looked fretfully from one to the other. He could not fail to be aware of the animosity between his son and the Westwoods. It was patent in every word uttered, but matters were going too fast for his thoughts to keep abreast.

"Do you not recollect, Sir Walter, that it occurred to me that the murderer might wish to do away with my sister? That the murderer might try to make her death look like suicide, as a result of a guilty conscience? To this end I insisted she not only be locked in her chamber, but that she shouldn't be alone at any time. I must confess, I didn't truly think Meg had any information, or I'd have her locked up as well, for her own safety. However, in doing what I did, I put Justin in danger, too, it was not inconceivable that the murderer might attack and kill him for the key, and then kill Mary. So, I recommended he locked his door, and open it to only those he trusted."

"But if he locked himself in, he held the key. So he could have got out again and released your sister, if he chose," protested Geoffrey Soames. He was aware something was going on, but not sure what.

"To what end?" The words came sharply from Hal. "We must begin by trusting someone. Did we not agree Justin Danvers was neutral in this matter of your cousin's death? That he, of us all, had nothing to gain?"

Geoffrey Soames snorted, but said nothing further, whilst Sir Walter turned to his wife, with an uneasy air. Lady Soames had been fidgeting through the proceedings. At first, Hal had put it down to nerves. It was indeed a trying episode for them all, but the other women had managed to remain calm. The amusement unwittingly provided by the village men had raised a few smiles, and unconsciously the ladies had relaxed. All, save Lady Soames, who was growing increasingly restless.

As the silence lengthened, Sir Walter nodded his head. "Yes, I think I understand, thank you, Mr Westwood."

"Guy Armstrong had escorted his sisters to their chamber. I now instructed my brother, Ned, to mount guard in that gallery," continued Hal. "For whilst it was agreed they were in little danger, and were, of consequence not locked in, it seemed good sense in view of the situation, to make sure they remained in their chamber all night."

"Actually, Hal, Mistress Cecily has told Justin earlier how she was wakeful in the night," said Ned.

"Yes," said Justin, "Mistress Cecily Armstrong has made a disposition and signed it later. In it she says that she sat in the gallery for half an hour last night, on the window seat overlooking the courtyard. As she can have little reason to wish either Sir Edward, or his serving wench ill, I don't think it significant she was alone at this time. She couldn't have left the gallery without being seen."

"She might wish Meg dead," interrupted Soames. "If her brother and his paramour killed my cousin, as is most likely, she could have decided to silence Meg. For 'tis plain she admires both adulterers."

There was an amazed silence at this accusation, followed by loud rebuttals, as both Hal and Guy expressed their annoyance.

Justin hastily stepped in. "Mistress Cecily, who barely tops my chest—take a knife and cut the throat of a strapping wench like Meg— who was at least three inches taller and several stone heavier?" he asked sarcastically. "I think it unlikely!"

"Libby, my wife had, as I have already said, retired with my son and his nurse," continued Hal, as Guy Armstrong glared at Soames. "They decided to sleep before the fire in her chamber, that being the warmer place, and she remained there until near dawn, when she came down the staircase to find me. For I, like Ned, sat up the night at the end of the Tower Gallery."

"Thus having untrammelled access to the outside of the house," Soames again interrupted.

"At this point, Ned, who'd come to consult with me on a certain matter, went down to the kitchens to see what information he could get from the servants there," continued Hal patiently.

"Leaving little Miss Cecily to run amuck, if she so chose," muttered Soames in a carping tone.

"Oh, for God's sake!" Guy Armstrong finally exploded with wrath. "If you can't talk sense, man, hold your damned viper's tongue. No, in fact, let's stop this fool play-acting, and shilly-shallying, and get to the crux of the matter! You explain yourself, Soames. You tell us why you really did meet with that wench last night."

Avis Soames lifted her head sharply, her wandering attention suddenly caught. "What did you say?" she cried, in a voice totally unlike her normal meek tone.

Justin's shrewd eyes moved to her gaunt, ravaged face

thoughtfully, "Mr Armstrong has pre-empted my request, for your son to give an account of the time he spent in the stables last night, Lady Soames," he replied, his voice carefully neutral, as he glanced swiftly about the hall.

"He wasn't in the stables," cried Lady Soames, her voice shrill. "He was in bed like a good Christian."

"Unfortunately, Mistress Cecily, who, we have established, was wakeful last night, observed Mr Soames from an upper window. He was seen entering the stable yard, at about half-past midnight," replied Justin concisely. "Neither, indeed, does your son deny he did so. He merely declines to state for what purpose, other than an apparent burning desire to see his horse, and great solicitude for the future of Sir Edward's mistress, he went hence, on what must be one of the bitterest winter nights any of us have ever known."

"I told you earlier, I admit making an assignation with this wench, but she never came," snapped Geoffrey. He had been sitting beside his father with the air of a man barely keeping his temper during this, and spoke through gritted teeth.

Lady Soames cried out in horror at his admission.

"You've carefully noted that, have you, Justin," asked Hal, his voice grim. "That Mr Soames admits a prior appointment with the murdered servant girl."

"Both that, and the fact that he declares she never arrived for the meeting," agreed Justin equably.

"Oh Geoffrey! How could you?" cried Lady Soames, anguish in her voice. "Haven't I always bidden you not to heed the lures of a harlot like that?"

"Madam," snapped Geoffrey sulkily. "Hold your tongue."

"My lord," urgently Lady Soames turned to her husband, "can't you exert your influence over this wild boy? I beg you, my lord, can you not see so clearly how he stands on the very edge of hell's pit? Make him heed you well. Make him turn aside from the evil course your cousin led him to."

"My love," Sir Walter gently laid his hands across her agitated ones. "Be you still, I beg. There are other matters, of greater importance, requiring our attention here."

"What can be of greater importance than the salvation of our son's soul?" she cried, angrily shaking off his restraining hand.

"As I see it, it comes down to this," said Guy Armstrong. He cast the woman an uneasy look and continued as if she didn't exist, "By his own admission Geoffrey Soames was the last of us to see this maid, Meg, alive. This was shortly after she'd told us all, she knew who killed Sir Edward. Now she's dead, too. And, it looks to me, as if Soames is the guilty party."

"I rather think that is somewhat over simplifying the matter, Armstrong," said Justin mildly.

"What does he say?" Lady Soames, her attention caught again, clasped her husband's arm, as if she could not comprehend the words going on about her.

"Armstrong, to cover his own guilty tracks, accuses me of killing the wench Meg, and by implication my uncle, too," snapped Geoffrey Soames, casting an angry look at Armstrong. "Be still, if you please, Mother."

"No! No, this is nonsense!" cried Lady Soames, loud in her horror. "Geoffrey is entirely innocent of such an evil crime. This woman was a harlot, a strumpet. The Lord struck her down."

"All are innocent until proved guilty, Lady Soames," said Justin patiently, as Hal eyed the woman askance.

"No, heed me. The jezebel never had time to meet with Geoffrey. He is yet uncontaminated. The Evil One came with his horns, and cloven feet, to carry her off to hell!" she cried.

Justin frowned, "What mean you exactly, ma'am?" he asked sharply. "Who never had time? Do you mean Meg, or your son?"

The woman's face was suddenly ashen. She darted a

sidelong glance from her husband and son, to Justin and Hal, and a cunning look came over her face. "She was a trollop and a jade," she declared. "Running after each and every man, like a bitch on heat. No husband, no, nor son, was safe from her wiles!" She turned in her seat, looking to the other women, who sat silent and puzzled by her behaviour.

"The girl's conduct is nothing to the point," said Justin slowly. He found her loud words, and odd actions, at a variance with her previous, decorous behaviour. "Madam, Lady Soames, answer me this, if you please. Did you meet with Meg last evening?"

"I? No, no!" she cried wildly. "Why should I sully myself with the like of that slut? Thoust cannot touch pitch and not be defiled."

"Possibly not," agreed Justin, his calm tones noticeable, beside her agitated manner. "So in effect, there is no foundation to your claim that Meg never had time to meet with your son?"

"She didn't, I tell you!" she cried, scarcely heeding his words, but angrily pushing aside her gentle husband's protest. "I saw her, aye, I watched her. Dressed up in all her finery she was. Ribbons in her hair; lace on her bodice; The slut! I saw her, strutting about, her hips swaying, trying to trap my son. I tell you, I'll not allow such things, now I am mistress here. This household will be very different from this day forth. Sluts and whores will all be sent from this place. Only the godly, in whom the good Lord rejoices, shall be allowed to remain. This will be a place of peace."

Justin met Hal's eyes, he raised his brows a little, wondering what he made of it. Was she responsible for the murder, he wondered? Or, was it more that the religious mania, always present in her mind, had suddenly spilled over into madness?

"Sir Walter, can you not verify that your wife was at your side all night?" he asked, hoping to settle the problem another way.

"Well, no, I cannot swear to it," replied Sir Walter uneasily. He glanced to his wife, who had subsided a little, although she was muttering, and still casting strange, wild glances about her, as if she were continuing a dispute with some person they couldn't see. A cold fear gripped his heart, as he realised she was going beyond his control. "You must understand, my wife spends a good while in prayer each evening. Sometimes, she is on her knees for as much as an hour or more, Mr Danvers." He hesitated, looking anxious and wretched. "I must confess last night I fell asleep, whilst she was still at her devotions. It had been a long, exhausting and emotional day."

"My lady," Hal leaned forward, fixing her wavering gaze with his piercing eyes, and attempted to hold it. "This low trollop, Meg," he began to talk to her in a light conversational tone, appearing by his manner and the way he moved, to exclude the remainder of those present. He hoped she might respond more rationally to an intimate conversation between two people, rather than this open enquiry. "This openly acknowledged harlot of your late cousin, as wicked a slut as I've ever laid eyes on, I must confess. Tell me now, was it not in your mind to punish her, as a divine instrument of the Lord's Holy Law?"

"No, I'll not have this," cried Geoffrey Soames, angrily jumping up. "I see your trick, Westwood. So intent are you on clearing your family, you'll do anything to incriminate mine."

"Indeed, Hal," Justin broke in doubtfully, mindful of the law.

Lady Soames interrupted, her eyes gleaming with fanatical light, "No, for Hal Westwood is right, my son. The wicked shall be punished! The unclean shall be cast forth! Think you there's not a sacrifice I wouldn't make for you? Have I not seen the way clear for your father? Do you not understand that he, a godly man, will bring peace and justice and ways of righteousness to this place, ousting the evil of Sir Edward? Never think I'd not have even greater care of you, my beloved. I'll protect you from evil now, even as I protected you from want as a child."

"What is your opinion, Justin?" hissed Hal. He watched Geoffrey came to his mother, forcing her back to her seat and dropping to his haunches beside her, and Sir Walter, as he tried to calm her. "Is she verging on madness, or hinting at the truth."

"It's impossible to tell," replied Justin gravely. "She could be mad—or just cunning. Either way, it'll be a devil to prove—and impossible, I guess, to bring to law."

"She's raving mad," said Guy Armstrong with conviction.

"I must admit she's much worse than last time she visited. Indeed, she's been getting steadily worse since she arrived," said Mary quietly.

"Yes," said Guy, "she's dangerous in my opinion, and should be confined."

"I agree with that at least," said Justin quietly as Lady Soames roughly pushed aside her husband's gentle hands, and embraced her son fervently.

"Sir Walter, do you not agree that this all seems a little too much excitement for your wife? Would she not, perhaps, be better in her chamber?" he suggested kindly.

"Aye, and under lock and key," added Guy grimly.

"In her chamber resting," continued Justin firmly. "Perhaps a physician could be summoned to attend her, once the thaw sets in. Forgive me, but it would appear her brain is a little inflamed, by all the troubles we have before us."

The relief was obvious in Sir Walter's face at this suggestion. He nodded his assent, and turned to her again, joining his son in gently urging her to this measure.

Lady Soames, however, would have none of his soothing, even brushing aside Geoffrey, as she sprang to her feet. "No, no, what mean you, ill? Sloth is what ails thee, my lord. The Lord protects those who do his work. I am not ill. There is much for me to do. The world needs cleansing of evil."

As Sir Walter fell back, a little dismayed, she strode across the hall, appearing to push up her sleeves, as if she would begin scouring at once. "Do not think I don't know what you are at. You seek to hinder me in my mission. You all think that, if you call me mad, you can go on with your wicked sinning. Take heed of what I say! The Day of Judgment may be closer at hand than you think! Look to your consciences! This time the Lord won't send his own Son again to redeem your sins. This time, he might call on one of your sons as sacrifice, as he did with Isaac." She pushed her way past Constable Drew in the doorway, and went out.

"There, I told you she's past help," muttered Guy, glaring at Justin. "She should be locked up for all our safety."

"I don't know that it might be for best, Sir Walter, for her own protection, as much as anything," suggested Justin quietly. He should have saved his breath, Geoffrey Soames immediately entered a caveat, and Guy Armstrong, reluctantly backed by Hal, began to dispute this loudly. A fine quarrel ensured and showed signs of lasting for hours, so that, at first, the sound of a scream almost went unheard.

Only Libby caught it crying, "Oh, but, hush! What was that?"

As if in reply, came a loud cry of fear. All looked to each other blankly, until Ned suddenly cried, "Cecily?"

Guy Armstrong, recognising the repeated sound, crossed the room with one bound, an oath on his lips, but Hal and Ned thrust the slow-thinking Zac Drew aside, and were through the low door before him.

Chapter Nineteen

From above came more screams of someone in both fear and pain, and a repeated begging for release.

"My God, that old witch has got Cecily," cried Guy Armstrong in horror. He followed the brothers up the stairs two at a time, with Justin coming, but a little in his wake.

The rest of the party rose, bewildered, staring after them. Geoffrey Soames suddenly raced to follow the other men, whilst the others hurried to stand open-mouthed at the foot of the staircase.

"She's taking her up the tower," cried Ned, whose fleetness had outstripped the other men. His voice drifted back down to them. "Dear God, what can she intend?"

"No harm, no harm," bleated Sir Walter, almost in tears. He advanced a few stairs ahead of the remaining women and the constable. "My lady has often said what a sweet, gentle child Mistress Cecily is. I swear to you an innocent like she cannot be in danger."

"Sir Walter, your wife is clearly unhinged," said Libby, her voice sharp in sudden fear. Suddenly recollecting all the talk of sacrifice of sons and Isaac, she pushed past him on the stairs. "All must be in danger from a mad woman! Hal, Hal, where is little Harry?"

"Never fear!" Hal's voice drifted back down the stone tower staircase. "Lady Soames has gone straight past him. He is safe. Both he and Alys are coming down to you now."

All now gathered in the upper hall, at the base of the tower staircase, Geoffrey Soames running back down to allow the nurse carrying the sleeping child past. He caught the heartfelt tones of Libby's, "Thank God!" as he bounded back up to join the others. They were gathered outside the stout, oaken door of the room at the very top of the tower, which Ned and Guy shared.

"Madam!" he called, as he came to a halt behind the other men, several steps from the top. "Madam? Mother! What are you doing?" He watched as Hal tentatively turned the huge, old lock and found it secured. "Where are you?"

"I am here, my son, doing the Lord's will," she replied, in honeyed tones through the thick wood. "Why have you locked the door on us and taken Mistress Cecily?" he asked sharply, as Cecily gave another fear-filled cry.

"I am commanded to have help in doing the Lord's will," she replied. "Who better to assist His purpose, than this sweet, little thing? Only the pure in heart can achieve eternal salvation. This dear child is the innocent lamb the Lord requires for sacrifice. He will smile upon her, and forgive us our many sins."

"Don't harm her," cried Ned, in anguish, as Cecily cried out again, sobbing in her fear. "I beg of you, my lady, let her go free! She is in great distress!"

"Let the sweet angel go, to fall into your lecherous arms?" she replied. "No, I'll keep her here. Unsoiled by the evil of you men. She can go to her Lord as pure as only the innocent can be."

Then, as Cecily gave a great scream of horror and fear, Guy Armstrong cried out in disbelief. "My God, she's killing her! Cecily! Cecily— my little—don't fear, I am here! I'll set you free! We must forget this talking, Ned, give me the aid of your strong shoulder, we'll have the door down, and drag the hag out."

"Wait!" cried Hal, as Geoffrey Soames redoubled his efforts to persuade his mother to release Cecily. "Justin, didn't you say your chamber window gave out onto the battlements and leads above the gallery? No, listen

Guy, if we can get Cecily out another way, all may yet be well. Only, we must take great care. Lady Soames is plainly mad. We mustn't do anything precipitate, which might panic her into endangering either Cecily's, or her own life."

"Do you truly think she'll harm her, Hal?" cried Ned in anguish, "Oh, Hal, let me knock the door down. There isn't time for this!"

"I'll go, and see if it can be achieved," said Justin. "If I lean out of my window and look up, I may be able to see what she's at."

"I'll come along with you. We are too crowded here anyway," said Hal. "Soames, keep your mother talking. Ned, I'm relying on you to stop Armstrong from doing anything foolhardy!"

Hal leapt down the stairs in Justin's wake, just as Guy, his patience at an end, began bodily throwing himself at the cross-banded door, alternately cursing Lady Soames, and commanding her to give him entry.

Quickly they went down the worn spiral stairs, and along a corridor to Justin's chamber. This was an apartment set into the thickness of the wall, which joined the tower to the main house.

"I've caught sight of Ned from this window quite a few times," said Justin as they crossed the chamber.

"And I noticed that these battlements just above are badly broken, and about to—Oh no, look, there is Lady Soames coming out of the tower window now, dragging poor little Cecily behind her."

In horror, they both squeezed into the tiny casement, in time to observe the older woman, who was dragging the bound and sobbing girl along the icy leads of the battlements. They came to halt where the battlements were most dangerous. Lady Soames, raised her hands, and uncovered head to heaven, midst the lightly falling snow. Cecily, meanwhile, was huddled in a terrified heap at her feet. She clung, with frantic fingers, to the snow-covered stones, and shivered with mingled terror and cold.

"Dear God, she is mad!" cried Hal, in horror as the woman, appearing to finish her prayer, broke into song, which the wind gusted away, with a scattering of snowflakes.

"What does she imagine she's doing?" demanded Justin in exasperation, as Lady Soames walked forward to the very edge of the wall overlooking the courtyard two floors below. "Oh, have a care! That stone is quite decayed!"

Hal struggled with the rusted catch of the casement, forced it wide open, and thrust his head out to look above, and to his right. "Yes, it looks possible." he said, almost under his breath.

"What is? My God, what are you at?" cried Justin in dismay, as Hal swung up lightly onto the deep widow sill, and began to slide his long legs out of the window.

"I'm going to get the girl, and Lady Soames, too, if possible," he grunted with the effort, realising as the wind whipped keenly through his doublet, just how cold it was.

"Don't be a fool! There's a sheer drop from here to the yard!" Justin cried in horror, as his eyes went down to the group of servants and village men, who, hearing the furore, had all hurried out in the worsening weather. They were gathered there in the trampled snow, their heads thrown back in astonishment, pointing and crying out in wonder and dismay at the sight before their eyes.

"I know, don't remind me," said Hal, his shoulders following the rest of him. "You might come to the window, Justin, and be ready to take hold of Cecily, if possible."

"Hal, don't do it!" he cried, as Hal dropped over the edge and disappeared from sight momentarily, with only his hands still grasping the central bar of the window, whilst his feet scrabbled to find a toehold in the stonework of the walls. "Hal, you'll kill yourself!"

Hal grunted again, as the wind whisked a flurry of icy snow into his face and eyes. He had but the one chance. He looked over his shoulder to where the mad woman, oblivious of him, was still addressing her prayers to a sullen sky, and encountered Cecily's terrified eyes. He smiled, in what he hoped was a reassuring manner, although the cold was already numbing his mouth and lips. Then reached out a long arm to grasp what appeared to be the one sound stone in the broken, ragged teeth of the battlement wall. It felt strong enough, and without giving himself time to further contemplate, either its strength, or the horror below, he put his toe on another foothold, and let go of the casement.

The searing pain in his shoulder told him he'd made a grave error of judgement, and, for a few seconds, there was blackness before his eyes, but, there was no help for it, and he forced his muscles into further action. With his other foot, he strove desperately to equalise his weight, and the now numbed fingers of his right hand came up to grasp whatever he could.

There was no time for indecision. Ignoring the shrieking pain of his wrenched muscles, he hauled himself between the stones, sending several spiralling down to the courtyard below, scattering the crowd. Their exclamations of horror were turned into a thin cheer of relief, which echoed up from below, as they saw he was safe.

"What the devil are you doing? Where's Hal?" Ned erupted into the chamber as Justin, half out of the casement, gave another cry of fear.

"No, it's alright, he's safe!" Justin called back over his shoulder, taking his eyes from Hal sprawled, breathing deeply on the leads, to look at Ned's ravaged face. "He's on the battlements. What's amiss?"

"I can't hold Armstrong. He's run mad!" cried Ned, as he thrust his head out of the window to see, with horror, Lady Soames haul Cecily to her feet, whilst Hal got to his knees. "Armstrong's beating down the door with a stool. Hal, Hal, have a care! Don't—don't frighten her—No! Oh, dear God, I thought they were going over then!"

"It's icy on those leads," cried Justin, who was clinging to the casement. His stomach was churning at the thought of the drop below. "Gently, Hal, remember the wicked, old harridan isn't in possession of her mind."

"Do you think I'd forget it?" Hal snapped, from chattering teeth as he stood upright, unsteadily. "Lady Soames, the wind is full chill out here, this evening.

Do, I beg, return from whence you came—before you both take cold."

"Nay, 'tis as soft as a lover's kiss on a summer morn," she cried, "Mistress Cecily and I shall bathe our faces in the May Day dew."

"Sweet Cecily, come you here," Hal extended his hand to the girl, who sobbed helplessly in terror.

"I cannot, sir," she whispered, through her icy tears, "My lady has me tied!"

To his horror, he saw that Cecily's bound wrists were attached to the gaunt waist of the mad woman, by her sash.

"I beg you, madam, set me free," Cecily sobbed piteously, and held out her hands.

Hal heard Ned's howl of rage and fear, which near drowned out Lady Soames's words. "Nay, nay, child, you don't want to go to him. I tell you, sweetheart, all men are wicked, evil, lust-filled creatures, who set traps for innocent maids. You come with me. Ignore the temptation of these devils. We'll sit at the feet of the Lord together!"

Hal, who'd advanced a few more steps along the treacherous ice of the broken leads, heard a commotion behind him, and much grunting, but didn't dare look back. He kept his eyes fixed on Lady Soames, who continued with her psalms, and looked about her at the view, as if she were taking the air on the May Day morn she clearly thought it was.

Closer and closer he edged, Cecily watching him with her sobs still coming, but silently, in desperation. Ned, red-faced with the exertion, swung himself to the battlements behind his brother as pieces of stonework fell below in his wake. Trembling, with her eyes riveted on the mad woman, Cecily extended her hands toward Hal, inch by inch, scarcely daring to breathe, lest this hope of rescue be snatched from her.

At that moment, the fusillade of banging, which had been an accompaniment to Lady Soames's song, ceased abruptly, and Guy Armstrong flung himself through the tower window, followed by Geoffrey Soames, whilst Sir Walter hovered in the background of the tower chamber calling for all to have a care.

Lady Soames, seeing the advance of the men, gave a cry of fear and stepped back as her feet slid from under her. The stones of battlement gave way, crashing down to the yard below again and she, with a shriek, slid over the edge in their wake.

Cecily, tethered to the woman by her sash, gave a scream, as she was jolted to the edge. Hal launched himself forward and caught her bodily to him and Ned, with a cry of terror, crashed forward, to fall on top of them both.

"Pull it up Ned, pull it up! Pull the sash, or she'll fall," cried Hal, who was trying frantically with fingers numbed by cold, to release the tightening knots, which bound Cecily.

Guy Armstrong arrived seconds later, pulled his dagger, and hacked through the sash. Once released, Cecily sobbed uncontrollably in his arms.

Hal got to his feet and hurried to help Ned, braced, as he was, against the crumbling stone; trying to haul the struggling, screaming, madwoman up the side of the rotting battlements.

Geoffrey Soames staggered past Guy and Cecily, to throw his arms about Hal's waist. They all struggled to keep their footing in the frozen snow and the fast-fading light. Sir Walter stood shivering and weeping alongside, beseeching his wife to stay calm.

"Give a hand, Armstrong," panted Hal. His injured shoulder was screaming in agony as slowly, inch by inch, the sash began to pull back over the broken edge of the battlement.

"Let her go!" Guy cried wrathfully, shaking his head in reply. " 'Tis naught but a mad woman, a murderess. The world will be a better place without her. Let her fall."

"Be she mad, or a murderess, the law will deal with her," said Justin, his teeth chattering with fear as he made his way light-headily toward them, tottering between churned up snow, fallen stones and broken leads.

"Come, Armstrong, put poor Cecily through the window. See, Libby is waiting to take her. For God's sake, give us the aid of your strength." He grabbed hold of Soames's waist, and hauled with all his might.

Grumbling under his breath, Guy pushed past Sir Walter, cradling the faint Cecily in his arms as he guided her to the safety of Libby's embrace.

Then, as he turned back to assist the others, Ned gave a cry of horror. "The silk! It's splitting! The rough edge of the stone is fraying the silk. Dear God, Soames! Catch at it!"

This last exclamation came as the sash finally split. The mad woman, with a long drawn-out scream, fell first against the castle wall with a sickening thud, and then plunged head long onto the snowy cobbles of the courtyard beneath.

"Get your father inside, Soames," said Hal, as Sir Walter, with a piercing cry fell to his knees, weeping. "Indeed, let us all get inside, out of this bitter cold. We can do no more here."

"Thank God, we don't have to go back the way we

came," murmured Justin thankfully, as they followed the forlorn figure of Sir Walter back through the window into the tower room.

Chapter Twenty

It was a grim-faced and subdued party that gathered before the roaring fire in the Great Hall a little later. The bloodied, broken body of Avis Soames had been picked up by the servants and put upon a hurdle awaiting laying-out, with her victims, in the chapel.

The remainder of the guests sat, exhausted by events, sipping mulled wine, and allowing the women to minister salves and bandages to their hurts.

Ned and Justin had cuts and bruises to both hands and legs from their struggles with the frozen stones. Guy Armstrong's shoulders were aching from the attack on the tower door, which now hung drunkenly on its hinges, but Hal was in the worst case. Now all sense of urgency was over, his injured shoulder was screaming in agony, which showed in the greyness of his face and tautness of his mouth.

"What a dreadful, horrible end," faltered Sir Walter ashen-faced and twitching.

"Oh, my poor, dear wife! Oh, that sweet, sainted lady!"

"Sweet, sainted lady, be damned!" cried Guy Armstrong hotly. "She was a dangerous lunatic, who killed your cousin, and his whore, and tried to kill my innocent little sister! Sweet, sainted lady? She was an evil, old harridan, who deserved to die. A pity she had so easy an end, I say."

"Aye, we noted your reluctance to assist," snarled Geoffrey Soames, "and your hurry to smear her name with murder! It's you that profit from her death, you, and your strumpet. Don't think I'll allow all this to be swept aside, and the blame put at my mother's door, now she's dead and can't defend herself. You had the most to gain, and I'll make sure all the details of this day are known far and wide. You are not going to get away with this piece of infamy, Armstrong."

"Gentlemen, less heat, if you please," said Hal. His pale face was etched with pain, as he sipped at a cup containing a noisome-looking brew, which his sister Mary had handed him.

"Less heat!" Soames rounded on the injured man, his teeth drawn back in a snarl. "Don't try to come the justice over me, Westwood! I'll not be deterred by you all closing ranks, although you might not live to see the day out, sitting there drinking that Borgia's brew."

"My son, my son, I comprehend your grief," Sir Walter remonstrated gently. "But try, I beg, for a little civility, if you please. Hal Westwood is a hero, but for whose intrepid head, and quick wits, we'd be facing a greater disaster. He tried his best to save both ladies, you know, at not an inconsiderable risk to his own life."

"More risk than you realise, Sir Walter," cried Libby. She was endeavouring to fashion, with hands that she couldn't stop shaking, a sling for her husband. "He dangled a hundred feet above that courtyard by an already injured shoulder, in an effort to stop Lady Soames! What could you have been thinking of, Hal, to take such a risk?"

"I didn't think about my shoulder, until it was too late," he replied. He drank off Mary's brew defiantly and sat up with a low groan, submitting to his wife's and sister's ministrations, as they settled a sling about his neck, and tenderly lifted his useless arm into it. "Until I let go of that casement, I never gave it a thought. Then, I was in such agony, that I knew if I didn't move swiftly, I'd be splattered across that courtyard!"

There was an abrupt silence, as all seemed to see again, the figure of Lady Soames, flattened against the bloody snow. Then as he began a halting apology, Cecily interrupted hastily, "I'm so very glad you were not, Mr Westwood, and I thank you from my heart for rescuing me. Are you still in great pain?"

"I'm afraid I was all too aware of the risk," shuddered Justin. He was still extremely pale himself, and smiled uncertainly at Bess, as Hal assured Cecily he hardly felt his shoulder now. "I fear I have no head for heights at all."

"Then you were doubly brave," soothed Bess, "for you went onto the battlements, in spite of your fear."

"Even if he did have to spew his guts in the privy after!" sneered Soames. "God, you Westwoods sicken me, with your heroism and nobility!"

"We Westwoods don't greatly care for you, either, Soames!" snapped Ned. He had Cecily's hand clasped fast in his own, and looked as if he'd never let it go again. "You're full of nothing, but threats and bluster. Don't think to throw us from the scent that way. Lady Soames was mad, and you both knew it!"

"Not knew it," bleated Sir Walter, as Soames turned from Ned's determined glare. "I had begun recently, I must confess to—to entertain the—the gravest of doubts—as to her sanity. Hadn't we, Geoff?"

"No!" Geoffrey snapped curtly. "No, my mother was

as sane as any of you. She may have been a little over zealous, mayhap, in matters of religion, but that is hardly a fault in these godless days. I shall take my affidavit she was sane enough, until literally tipped over the edge, by you mad pack of Westwood dogs, baying for her blood!"

"Come, Soames! I can understand your horror and grief," said Justin, "but to try to whiten your mother's actions thus, is criminal! Sir Walter, I shall require a deposition from you, stating that your wife's sanity had recently become suspect. I shall hand that, along with my report of findings into this matter, to the sheriff and crowner, as soon as this snow thaws. I imagine the case will rest there."

"Yes, yes, indeed," said Sir Walter hastily. "No, Geoff, leave it. I beg—no more this night—I beg you. Let us both retire with our grief."

Surprisingly, Soames made no further protest, but got up abruptly and left the hall. Sir Walter got to his feet hesitantly. "Do you think the findings will preclude a Christian burial, Mr Danvers?" he asked piteously.

Justin glanced blankly to Hal, who stared at the wine in his cup. "I can't see why, Sir Walter," he replied at last. "The lady slipped, did she not?"

He bowed his head. "Thank you gentlemen, thank you," he said quietly and followed his son from the room.

"Do you truly believe so, Hal?" asked Ned.

Then, as Hal shrugged and drank off the mulled wine, Libby said gently, "It seemed to me, she wanted to die. She made no effort to help herself, in fact, quite the reverse, poor woman."

Ned nodded. "Yes, she was screaming foul abuse at me, and trying to pull off the cord about her waist, all the time we were struggling to haul her back." He gave a sudden shudder, as he recollected her mad eyes. "But she deserved to die, trying to kill Cecily as she did!"

"Will that be the end, do you think, Danvers?" Guy Armstrong asked anxiously, as he refilled Hal's wine cup. "Do you truly think she killed Sir Edward, and the girl Meg?"

Justin sighed. "I don't think we could have got a conviction on her confession," he admitted. "She was quite clearly mad, yet, if not her, who?"

"I thought it was Soames," said Ned.

"Perhaps, in which case, she'd have gladly died for him," replied Justin. "I don't know about Sir Edward, but I think she killed the wench. Most certainly she would have happily taken Mistress Cecily to her death.

In truth, Armstrong, it was a better end perhaps, than the horror of a trial, and either hanging, or being shut up in Bedlam for life."

Guy Armstrong shrugged. "This result doesn't clear either Mary, nor I, from suspicion. And in the future we've still Soames, and his dissatisfaction and complaints to contend with. He'll not let matters rest."

"Oh, I think he will," said Hal, grimacing in pain, as he moved slightly. "I think Sir Walter will find a way of persuading him." He met the others' blank eyes. "Sir Walter was rather concerned over the burial, don't you think?"

"You mean, we can always threaten to tell the authorities she took her own life?" Guy said, enlightenment breaking on his puzzlement. "Of course, if she's a suicide, she wouldn't be allowed a Christian burial."

"I don't think we need be quite that crass." Hal frowned at this spelling out in words that which he would much rather have left unspoken. He drank deeply of the wine, and felt the warmth finally coming back into his bones, with some relief.

"Yes," said Justin thoughtfully, "I think we'll tell Sir Walter, we'd best leave justice to the Lord, who sees so much more than we do, and knows well the secrets of our hearts."

"Speaking of secrets," said Guy, observing how Bess sat beside her husband, with her head on his shoulder, and gazed adoringly at him. "Are we to gather that your wedding is no longer to be concealed, Mistress Bess?"

"Well, of course, it isn't," said Mary firmly. "Fill Hal's cup again Guy. We'll all drink a toast to their happiness! Hal knows there is little point in continuing a senseless quarrel."

Hal felt a curious lassitude stealing over him. The pain was still in his shoulder, but not quite so fierce, and a pleasant warmth and muzziness surrounded him. "Indeed, I do Mary," he said, his words a little slurred. "I know, of all the people in the world I can trust, my new brother-in-law must rate highly. I merely hope the next brother-in-law you mean to present me with, won't try to get me drunk each occasion we meet. You are prepared to carry me to bed, are you, Armstrong?"

"Both you and your sister," he replied with a grin. "But if you are enquiring as to when we mean to be married, the answer is at once, privately, as soon as the rector can get here. My son won't be born a bastard, never fear."

"But the scandal, Guy," protested Fanny, looking horrified. "I beg you won't involve Tom in it."

"Tom is involved up to his neck," he replied. "He

married Bess and Justin on Christmas Eve. If there's going to be one great scandal anyway, we may as well give the gossips something to really get their teeth into."

Hal gave a tipsy laugh, "I rather fear, Mistress Armstrong, you are destined to a life of disappointment, if you cannot live with scandal. It appears you will probably be related to the Westwood family twice over, and we Westwoods cannot, it would seem, exist without scandal."

"Hal!" Ned's ruddy face flushed deeper with gratification, "Does that mean you'll back me with father, in my desire to marry Cecily?"

"Having gone to such lengths to rescue her, should we lose her to another?" Hal asked with a lazy laugh. "In truth, beside the furore that will be caused by Bess and Justin, and Mary and Guy, I think your betrothal and a marriage will be a shining example of the normal. Apart from that, if we can get you settled, Ned, that only leaves Hetta for our father to find an unpleasant surprise for. It seems, after all, he must be satisfied with one of us wedding an heiress!"

"I rather think, my dear, you've had too much of Guy's wine. I fear it might take two, or three, to get you to bed," said Libby, smiling, but with a faint air of disapproval.

"No, my dear," he returned her smile. "On the contrary, I've had just enough wine to see clearly, how lucky we are to be here this night. I raise my cup—A health to us all!"

Read the Last Chapter
of the First Book in the
Hal Westwood Restoration Mystery
Series:

A Flutter in the Dovecote
Set in England in the Summer of 1660

Conclusion

Chapter 25

It was very late in the day, and long after all the fuss had died down, that Sheriff Hughes had finally consented to believe the evidence of his eyes. Mr Fenton had done marvelling over the inequity of Will Longstaffe and both had declined to take supper with them. A weary group of people sat in the soft twilight. They did not talk so much now, but seemed to reflect on the drama of the day.

There was a long pause and they'd all declared they'd talk no more of it that evening when Aunt Margery asked, "Tell me, Justin, how was it you said none knew where the dagger had been found? I knew, so did Kate."

"I think almost everybody knew, ma'am," replied Justin ruefully. "I was merely hoping and praying Will might not know that we knew! You see, we had absolutely nothing against him that we could prove. I was trying desperately to trick him into admitting he had killed Mr Henry Westwood."

"None of it would have stood up in a court of law, young man," remarked Francis, who sat by his wife, lazily drinking a cup of wine.

"No sir, I am very aware of that. I was trying to get him to confess. A confession was the only hope we had! That or the end we did get." He hesitated, his eyes going past Margery to the soft evening beyond. "Perhaps the way it ended was better for all concerned."

"Certainly neater for us, although I'm not sure Sheriff Hughes will ever be convinced we didn't have a hand in it somewhere. He would have sooner found me guilty," said Francis, reflectively.

Margery sighed. "I cannot think why we did not see it earlier. After all we knew Will Longstaffe was Uncle Henry's—"

"Bastard," Ned supplied the word as she hesitated. Then as Hal stared, he added, "Oh, did you not know?"

Justin closed his eyes in disbelief. "Are you saying, Ned, you knew all along?"

"Yes, didn't all of you? I thought everyone knew."

Justin was forced to resist the impulse to smack Ned's head and Hal sat looking stunned. "That was why he hated me so! Do you think it was he my uncle had named as heir in his earlier will?"

"I think it likely. Did Mr Fenton not tell you your

Uncle Henry said he'd never leave this land for his brother to ruin? And that his will would set the cat amongst the pigeons?" Justin asked quietly.

"Or even set up a flutter in the dovecote," Hal smiled sadly at the aptness of it. "So all Will's love for my uncle turned to hate and he killed his own father."

Justin nodded. "So it would seem. Alas, we have no proof of this, and so it must remain idle speculation, as Sheriff Hughes took great pains to point out. Like him, I doubt the horse coper's testimony, if he could be persuaded to give it, would stand up. And that was if we could track down the man from Ross. I imagine the gentleman's horse is long gone. I think Will was hoping Hal would prove unsuitable. Had he not said Hal would be little better than a fop or a fool? Perhaps he was hoping you'd refuse to marry the heiress your uncle had chosen. Who can say? Then, when you proved neither a fool nor difficult, he was set to teach you. It must have seemed an insult."

"I can well understand his hatred of me," agreed Hal.

"Never forget he killed his father, your uncle, in cold blood. He then did his best to make it look as if your father was guilty, and would, but for the King's Grace, have seen him hanged for murder. I don't think he would have stopped there either. I think you'd have been the next target, and finally as you'd wavered in your allegiance, Ned, you would have followed."

"This is foolish!" cried Hal, "Mayhap it all happened as you say, but to kill Ned and I? No, it cannot be! Did he think none would suspect?"

"Once a murderer has killed successfully his confidence grows and begins to know no bounds," Justin replied. "I don't suppose you'd have suffered a dagger in the heart, Hal. No, yours most likely would have been an accident—out riding perhaps? Then the tale would go round that the Westwoods were cursed, to prepare the way for Ned's end. Don't you see? He was close to you all, so his opportunities were endless."

"It is as well you've thought it all out, Mr Danvers, for that Sheriff Hughes had little idea. He seemed very confused I thought," said Aunt Kate with a look of admiration for Justin.

"As well he may," agreed Francis.

"Bah! That odious man! I do not know why he is allowed to come here! If I were mistress of Westwood, I would have never let him set foot in the place again!" cried Jacqueline.

"I very much doubt he ever will, Jacqueline, so Libby need not consider it," Hal's words came sharply.

"*Bon!*" she replied, ignoring this barb. "Me, I am relieved in my mind by this assurance, now we may all sleep sounder in our beds!"

"Not you and I, my lovely," said Francis. He had subjected his son's shadowed face to a thoughtful stare for some time, now he spoke out. "At least only for this one night. Tomorrow we are off on our travels again."

"Travels? What is this?" she demanded, turning to stare at him.

"I have a little business to transact in Holland and then we shall travel on to Paris for a while. Perhaps we shall stay all the summer, perhaps longer, who can say?"

"*Paris! Bon!*" Jacqueline cried with delight as she clapped her hands. "Now you tell me something I like. But how is this, Francis? First you say I must come to England to make the home for your daughters, now you say we must go to France!"

"Yes, you'll be better there, where I can keep an eye on you," Francis murmured, his eyes veiled. He hadn't needed the hints Margery had insisted on dropping into his ear not half an hour since. He could tell from the manner in which Jacqueline looked at Hal's wife there was trouble in the air. He was a fool, he supposed, to have brought home so young and lovely a wife. He'd imagined at first it wouldn't matter. A young man often fell in love with his new step-mother, if she was young and pretty enough. Provided that woman was one of character, no harm need be done, but Jacqueline was a different kettle of fish. He'd seen as soon as he arrived Hal was uneasy in her presence. And when he'd spoken to him of it there had been something different in his manner. There was an awkwardness in the way Hal talked, which had never been there before. It was obvious she was up to her usual tricks, and it would be better to remove her from where she could make the sort of mischief she so delighted in. He must leave his son to make his way in peace with his young wife.

Jacqueline had been thinking over his words and had not liked the inherent criticism implied in them. "What of your daughters? Where are they to go?"

"In the batch of letters, which arrived from London the other day, I received a letter from Mr Eustace agreeing terms for Jane's dowry," Francis replied. "There is no reason the wedding can't go forward as planned in the autumn. Hal has said he will attend to all the details. In the meantime, Jane will return here to keep company with Bess." His slightly amused glance travelled to Justin, who, he noted, had been careful to select a seat at some distance from his love. "As to sweet Bess's fate, I cannot say. None has yet made her an offer."

Justin's head came up at this, his eyes flying to the older man's face. "Is one given to understand, sir, that you have abandoned your search for a great match for Bess?"

Francis grinned. "I'll admit I don't think I could find one better that the one staring me in the face. Young man, you've saved what reputation I had left to me. I am weary of the task of finding suitable husbands for my daughters. If you want her, she's yours!"

"Father!" protested Hal as he got to his feet. Libby turned to him in consternation, certain his dislike of Justin would prevent this hoped-for union. "Sir, is that not an offhand way in which to present so lovely a jewel to one to whom you owe your life and honour?"

Hal went to where Bess sat, taking her hand and making her rise, too, as he turned to confront Justin.

"Justin, as a family we owe you much. More than we could ever repay you. We are glad to consent to your betrothal to Bess, secure in the knowledge that she'll find a good and gentle husband in you."

Libby clasped Hal's sleeve as Bess took Justin's hand, her eyes starry. "Oh, Hal, thank you, thank you!" she whispered.

"Tell your father to write to Hal, young man. He'll pass the letter on to my lawyer to settle everything,"

Francis said, as his sisters sighed contentedly. Both Margery and Kate had been loud in praise of Libby's brother and not backward in hinting at his reward.

Francis's eyes travelled to Ned, who was looking in patent disgust from Bess and Justin to Hal standing with his arm about Libby's waist, as she congratulated her brother. "Well, young Ned, have you had enough of these lovers? Will you throw in your lot with me and come adventuring?"

Ned looked to him, his eyes bright, plainly drawn by the prospect. Then as Hal, his attention caught by the question, turned to look, he shook his head decidedly. "No sir," he said simply. "I can't do that! I've to stay here and help Hal. We agreed it earlier. He says now Will Longstaffe is gone, he'll need me more than ever!"

"Is that so?" asked Francis in surprise. "Am I to leave all my children in your care, Hal?"

"Libby and I would be honoured if you would do so, sir. And I can think of no better place for them to be, than here at Westwood Hall."

❧

Read the First Chapter
of the next book in the
Hal Westwood Restoration Mystery
Series:

A Trip to Jericho

Set in the Summer of 1665

Chapter One

Hal Westwood paused glancing rapidly about the court-yard. He was a stones throw from Lincoln's Inn, but a hundred miles from it in spirit. His heart sank abruptly, and he pushed his way through the squalor to the house where a lop-sided sign proclaimed: STEENE AND JOHNSON, ATTORNEYS AT LAW.

The entrance was dank, narrow, and the room he entered only a little better, having a stained, flag floor, dark panelling and the distinct odour of rot.

A bent, balding man looked up from a desk, blinking as he took in the prosperous air of his master's latest visitor, seeing a tall, handsome, dark young man, well dressed, although not in the excessive fashion of the court, with an air of one well-used to command in his eyes.

"Mr Danvers?" he asked, "Can you tell me where I'll find Mr Justin Danvers?"

"Danvers?" replied the man, his high opinion of the

visitor falling abruptly. "He is working in the chamber above, but surely a gentleman like yourself would rather see our principal Mr Johnson? Or, if you could come back tomorrow, perhaps even Mr Steene himself might oblige."

"No, I thank you," replied Hal pleasantly. "My business is with Mr Danvers, and is purely personal."

"Danvers is not permitted personal callers," said the chief clerk flatly. "He's not a partner, you know. Indeed 'tis only the goodness of Mr Steene's heart which—"

"Yes, I do know," interrupted Hal sharply, "and if Mr Danvers isn't permitted personal callers, I'll seek his professional advice. Pray, tell him I am come."

The clerk sniffed audibly, "I'm not an errand boy," he muttered. "He is in the first chamber to the left, at the head of the stairs."

Hal's eyes lingered reprovingly on the man's pinched face for a few seconds, in a manner which, those who had occasion to come before the Bench these past few years, had reason to remember. Like them, he squirmed mentally, and hastened to open the door for Hal, bowing in an obsequious manner.

"At the top of the stairs sir!" he said quickly. "Do take care of the third stair. The rats have eaten best part of it away."

Hal mounted the stairs, observing the rat holes grimly, feeling the heat rising with him in the narrow space. The door stood open wide at the head, and the windows likewise, in the room beyond, but no breath of air came to relieve his heated brow.

"Hal?" Justin Danvers brought to the doorway by the footsteps, stared in amazement. "Hal! Is it truly you?"

"Justin, —at last!" Hal grasped his hand. "By heaven, you've led me a merry dance across London! I'd have never believed anyone could disappear so effectively."

"It was relatively easy," returned Justin, his eyes wary as he recollected himself, after his surprise. "Once one gives up all pretence to gentility, life is easily anonymous."

Hal, entering the chamber in his wake, turned to look at him as the full light of the summer's afternoon fell upon his young face, and he was shocked. Gone was the confident young fellow of last Christmas-tide at Sidworth Castle. Instead, a hollow-eyed, thin-faced man, with lank hair, and shoulders bent with care, looked back at him.

"Justin, are you ill?" he asked in concern.

"I've had the fever," he conceded. "There's a mite of it about, and plague, too, so they say."

"But you are so thin, and pale," said Hal, his voice echoing his shock.

"Aye, lack of food does that," retorted Justin, "and sixteen hour days working in this place." He laughed bitterly, and coughed in a disquieting manner, as if it were habitual.

"Sixteen hours a day?" said Hal in dismay.

"I start at six and finish, on average, at ten," he replied wearily. "What can I do for you? Please sit."

Hal took the unsteady chair gingerly. "Bess, she is well? Where is she?"

"She is not far from here, in Rankin's Court," said Justin, his face stony. "She is well enough," he hesitated, then added, "She expects our child in the autumn."

"Bess is to have a child!" cried Hal, then glancing about him added, "Here?"

"Where else is there," said Justin impatiently, "Many are born in the city you know."

"Aye," said Hal grimly, "and a few even survive! Come home, Justin."

Justin's jaw set. "This is my home," he said waving his hand in the direction of the sooty rooftops.

"No," Hal shook his head, "this is nobody's home. This is the mouth of hell, and only your stubborn stupidity keeps you here! Why didn't you come to us when you fell out with your father? Why run off in that dramatic fashion, leaving Libby mad with worry?"

"I had no right to lay my troubles on your doorstep. You no more approved the match than your father," he replied.

"You lie. Justin," he said hotly. "I swore to give you my support at Sidworth Castle."

"Aye, when you were drunk," retorted Justin flushing. "After Mary had given you herbs to sooth your shoulder, and Armstrong fed you enough wine to mellow your censorious disapproval of their affairs."

"I admitted I'd been wrong," snapped Hal. "Did I not say so before all of you? Did we not plan how to get my father to agree to both yours, and Ned's marriages?"

"Yes! We planned it and it went awry on my father's meanness," he replied bitterly.

"He's dead, you know, Justin," said Hal, in more gentle tones, as he recollected his errand.

"Yes, I know," said Justin. "Old man Steene told me. One of his cronies told him—and all about the marriage my father made before that!"

Hal nodded, casting his feathered hat to the table, and unbuttoning his coat. "No doubt, you found that as difficult to believe, as we did," he said evenly.

"Difficult to believe?" echoed Justin, with a bitter laugh. "Aye, I did, at first I was thunderstruck, then, when I thought about it more, I understood. He was hoping for another son, so he could completely cut me out."

"And he may yet do so," said Hal crossing his booted feet, "Mistress Johanna is with child."

"So I understand," he said bitterly. "There's no fool like an old fool!"

Hal smiled faintly, "How old was your father, Justin?"

Justin shrugged, "Fifty, fifty two, why?"

"My father has recently attained his sixtieth year, yet he still speaks hopefully of another son."

"He may speak hopefully, but 'tis many years since he sired a child. Hetta is fifteen, and Jacqueline has never had a pregnancy, has she? Tell me, is it true, as they say, my father's widow is a trollop?"

"One couldn't call her a trollop, Justin," said Hal, "not in all fairness! She is, to all intents, a respectable widow. Not exactly a gentlewoman, but nothing, truly, to blush for, I assure you. Indeed, even Libby agrees, she appears good-hearted enough, and she certainly made it her business to keep your father happy whilst he lived."

"Only he didn't live very long," said Justin. "What is

wrong with her?" he added shrewdly.

"Do you know, I couldn't say," cried Hal, sounding surprised. "I mean, she is all I've said, and yet, and yet something's not right! She's not bad, I don't think, and certainly not simple. If anything, rather sharp; in a cunning sort of way. Yet still, she's not right. She makes me uneasy."

"Do you mean she's—she's mad?" asked Justin, looking dismayed.

"No, no, not at all! I don't mean that, I mean she— she is a bit of a mystery. She lacks something—scruples, I suppose. Yes, that's what makes me uneasy. I think she'll stop at nothing."

"Nothing, do—do you mean—murder?" asked Justin quickly.

"No, no I don't," said Hal. "Such a thought never occurred—well hardly. Only it was rather odd, but I suppose I just dismissed her as a designing sort of female."

"I knew that as soon as I heard of her, and had it confirmed when I saw the will!" replied Justin dryly.

"Yes, that was odd!" agreed Hal unhappily. "You see your father came out to Westwood from his home at Adamsholme towards the end of January, just before he married, to tell Libby of the new will he'd made out. In it he said he'd left Mistress Johanna an adequate jointure, even though she'd had no dowry. He left everything else to Libby, house, business, money, trusting to her good sense to see everything properly bestowed. We took it as meaning that he wanted Libby to see Mistress Johanna wanted for nothing, and I privately believe he was asking her to make everything right with you for him, if you should not be reconciled. But then, when he did die, this new, totally different will appeared, which, it seems, he signed in the few days he was ill. He sent for a notary, and signed it there and then."

"So it is completely legal!" sighed Justin.

"I fear so," said Hal, "I do believe in his weakened state, he may have been coerced into signing it. You must understand, neither Libby, nor I were sent for, even though he was ill for some days. But what I can't understand is this: why didn't she take everything in that case? Why still leave the house and business to Libby, in trust to the child, if it were a boy?"

"Because that way, she'll get it all. And we'd not think of contesting it. If she'd been greedy, we most certainly would have done so, but now, don't you see, if the child is a girl, or still-born, she'll have a handsome fortune to walk away with, which she probably will get anyway!"

"So, why didn't you come home to contest it?" asked Hal. "It's taken me three months to track you down."

"Come home, to what?" demanded Justin, "To become my sister's pensioner."

"You arrogant fool!" cried Hal angrily. "You know Libby better than that! She needs you. Your step-mother has this rascally rogue, her cousin, she says—her lover, is nearer my guess—and he's playing ducks and drakes with the business your clever brain made ten-times more successful!"

Justin's head came up at that, "How is it Johanna is still there?" he asked.

"Because who else would run the business? Libby herself?" asked Hal. "No, she's waiting for me to find the fittest person, her brother."

"I'm sorry, I have employment," Justin replied with some arrogance.

"Aye, I can see how delightful it is," said Hal, his tone cutting as he rose to his feet, "Where will I find Bess?"

Justin rose also, "She is—she is unsettled in her mind, at this time, Hal. I pray you won't distress her."

"I distress her?" he replied coldly. "What mean you, Justin? Do you fear I'll try to keep her in squalor and poverty in this city for my own vain glorious ends, rather than bring her to safety and security, in the heart of her family in the country?"

Justin hunched a shoulder. "She's in Rankin's Court, across the square," he snapped.

Hal stood up. "I calculate I've had thirty minutes of your time. Whom do I pay? You, or the clerk below?"

"I'll deal with it," snapped Justin.

"Indeed you'll not," returned Hal coldly. "If you can take nothing from me, I'll take nothing, not even bad advice from you. Good afternoon."

Printed in the United States
23523LVS00001B/47